여로의 끝

2020 아르코 창작산실 연극 대본 공모 선정작

여로의 끝

이지훈 한영판 희곡집

평민사

차례

서문 ||||||||||||||||||||||||||||||||||||||||||||||||

셰익스피어 선생
양해도 구하지 않고 내 멋대로 당신의 말년 삶을 그려보았어요.
450년 전이라 뭐 남아 있는 기록도 없고
알려진 사실은 그저 한 줌.
사람들은 알고 싶었고 전기(傳記)는 수도 없이 많이 나왔죠.
당신 작품에 대한 책들도 큰 도서관 한 층이 모자랄 정도로 차
고 넘쳐요.
그냥 한 남자, 어린 시절에 남편 아버지가 되어 버린
그래서 집을 나가 인생을 던져 봤던 남자, 그 남자가 궁금했답
니다.
껄껄 웃을지도 모르겠어요,
아니면 눈살을 찌푸리실까?
당신이 자료들을 맘대로 주무르며 작품을 썼듯이
나도 당신처럼 그렇게 했다고 말해야겠어요.

스트랫포드 에이번 강가에
쓸쓸히 앉아 있는 늙은 남자

런던 글로브 극장 마당의 함성 소리 떠올리고 있나요?

팬찮아요.

다 떠나고 텅 빈 극장

앤도 주디스도 당신 곁에 있는데요

그리고 온 세상 극장에는 당신이 만들어 놓은 인물들이

오늘 밤에도 무대 위에서 표효하고 있고

사람들 혼을 쏙 빼놓고 있잖아요,

누구에게나 "여로의 끝"은 다가오죠.

잘 맞아야죠.

이지훈

2023 9.16

여로의 끝

등장인물

앤 (Anne)
수잔나 (Susanna)
주디스 (Judith)
마가렛 휠러 (Margaret Wheeler)
메리 (Mary)
조운 (Joan)
산파
하녀
윌 (Will)
존 홀 (John Hall)
토마스 퀴니 (Thomas Quiney)
사우스햄튼 백작 (Southampton)
변호사
목소리(V.O)
지바뀌 새

시간 : 1613-16년
장소 : 영국 스트랫포드(Stratford-upon-Avon), 런던
구성 : 1막 5장/ 2막 3장/ 3막 5장

윌리엄 셰익스피어의 아내 앤은 58세다. 큰딸 수잔나는 31세로
남편 닥터 존 홀과의 사이에 딸 엘리자베스(5세)를 두고 있다.
작은딸 주디스는 29세다.

작가노트

인물의 이름 뒤 대사 없이 비어 있는 여백은 침묵을 뜻하고 배우
는 이 침묵의 공간을 눈빛, 표정, 제스처, 몸짓 등 비언어로 표현
해야 한다.

[1막]

〈1장〉

검은 옷을 입은 세 여자.

앤은 발목까지 내려오는 긴 코트를 입고 한 손에 흰 시폰 스카프를 들었다. 큰딸 수잔나는 발이 덮이는 소매 없는 원피스를 입고 허리에는 광택이 있는 검은 에나멜 벨트를 둘렀다. 작은딸 주디스는 발목이 드러나는 스커트에 상의는 시수르(see-through)의 블라우스를 입고 컬러풀한 모자를 쓰거나 짧은 스카프를 머리에 두르고 있다. 발은 맨발이다.

타악이 섞인 선율에 맞춰 세 여인은 각자의 개성과 성격이 표현되는 움직임(춤)으로 빠르게 혹은 느리게 움직인다.

한 남자(윌)가 세 여자들 사이로 걸어 들어간다. 손을 뻗어 그들을 잡기도 하고 그들로부터 뿌리침을 당하기도 하며 엮이다 풀어지다를 반복한다. 그는 목에 흰 러플이 달린 17세기 스타일의 검은 색 짧은 윗도리를 입었다. 윌은 흰 종이에 시를 척척 휘갈겨 써서는 공중으로 날린다. 흰 종이는 눈처럼 위로 날아오르다가 무대 위로 떨어진다. 이 모습이 무대 뒷벽 전면 스크린 위에 나타난다.

앤은 나이가 들었지만 아름답고 기품이 있다. 왼손과 팔이 경직되다가 심히 떠는 증상이 가끔 나타난다.

수잔나   (휘날리는 종이 하나를 집는다. 읽는다)

시인, 사랑에 빠진 자, 광인,

모두 상상력으로 가득 찬 자들.

시인의 눈은

보이지 않는 걸 본다.

하늘에서 땅을 보고

땅에서 하늘을 보고

그 땅과 하늘 사이

상상력으로 채운다.[1]

주디스   (종이 하나를 집어 들고 읽는다)

상상력으로

시인의 펜은

텅 빈 것에 이름을 지어주고

존재의 자리를 잡아 준다.[2]

주디스   (읽은 종이를 머리 위로 높이 던져 버리고 또 하나를 집어 든다)

인간이란

저마다

활개치고 제 잘난 척하다

제 시간 지나면 퇴장하는

---

1) 〈한여름 밤의 꿈〉, 5.1. 7-17.
2) 〈한여름 밤의 꿈〉, 5.1. 7-17.

무대 위 배우.

앤   (바닥에 떨어진 종이를 한 장 집어서 읽는다. 놀라서 그 자리에
멈춰 선다. 왼손을 떨기 시작한다. 다 읽고는 종이를 머리 위로
던져 버린다)
사랑을 속삭일 때 남자는 4월 봄 날씨
결혼하고 나면 12월 겨울 날씨[3]

어릴 때 한 결혼은
인생을 망친다.[4]

수잔나   (읽은 종이를 머리 위로 던져 버리고 또 하나를 집어 든다)
천만년 후에도
내 연극은 계속 무대에 오르리라.
아직 생기지도 않은 나라에서
아직 알려지지도 않은 언어로.[5]

윌   (종이를 계속 위로 뿌리며)
나를 봐
나를 봐

---

3) 〈좋으실 대로〉, 4.1. 147-148.
4) 〈끝이 좋으면 다 좋다〉, 2.3. 298.
5) 〈줄리어스 시저〉, 3.1. 111-113.

나를 봐

거울로 세상을 비춰봐,

인생은 연극

무대는 거울에 비친 세상.

앤 (자기 머리 위로 날아오는 종이를 얼떨결에 한 장 잡는다. 손이

계속 떨린다)

여자는 언제나 연상의 남자를 취해야 해.[6]

모든 비밀 결혼은 비극으로 끝난다.

주디스 (종이를 한 장 집는다)

예를 갖춘 신성한 혼례식을 올려라.

만일 그 전에

처녀의 매듭을 푸는 일이 있다면

하늘이 내리는 축복의 감로수는 없으리라.

언짢은 눈살로 서로 쏘아보며

증오만 쌓게 되리

부부의 침실에는 잡초만 무성하여

둘은 합방을 피하고

자식들은 태어나지 못하리라.[7]

수잔나 (나르는 종이를 한 장 잡아 읽는다)

축복받은 결혼은

---

6) 〈십이야〉, 2. 4. 29-30.

7) 〈태풍〉, 4.1. 14-22.

아버지의 허락

아버지의 축복

그리고 많은 지참금.

윌   세상은 극장이고, 극장은 세상이다.

글로브(Globe)극장은 이 지구, 이 세상,

극장 속에 극장이

그 극장 속에 또 극장이 있다.

수잔나   희박한 공기 속으로

안개가 짙어진다.

아무 것도 보이지 않아

우리 셋 어디서 다시 만나지?

주디스   천둥, 번개, 빗속에서?

앤   (마지못해 입을 연다) 우리 셋 언제 다시 만나지?

주디스   내일, 내일, 내일?

수잔나   우리 셋 누굴 다시 만나지?

주디스   시인, 배우, 광인,

앤   남자, 무정한 연인, 늙은이.

수잔나   옛날 옛날에

한 어리고 철없는 사내애

연인을 버리고 가버렸네

기다리고 기다리다

여인은 홀로 늙어버렸네

주디스   시간은 폭풍이 몰아치고 땅이 갈라질 때도 어김없이 흘러가네.

사랑하던 여인의

아름답던 모습

어디로 갔나?

초여름 이슬처럼 사라졌네.

어린 딸들이 자라

아름답고 성숙한

그 여인으로 변했네.

월   모든 비밀 결혼은 비극으로 끝난다.

무대 뒤 전면에 갑자기 검붉게 불타는 런던 글로브극장의 모습
이 나타난다.

지붕이 불타며 무너져 내리고 기둥이 쓰러진다. 앤과 주디스 놀
라 사라진다. 월 셰익스피어 무대 중앙으로 나와 우두커니 선다.
믿을 수 없는 광경에 얼어붙었다. 장면 2장으로 이어진다.

〈2장〉

런던

1613

글로브극장 앞

월　네 시간은 끝났다.

무대 위 아무리 활개치고 제 잘난 척해도

시간 지나면 퇴장해야 하는 배우.

네 시간은… 끝났다.

(사이)

백치가 지껄인 이야기를 안고,

극장이 저렇게 사라진다…

보잘 것 없는 걸음걸음으로

하루, 또 하루를 달려왔는데…

마지막 순간, 여로의 끝까지

이렇게 달려왔는데

내일, 내일, 내일은 없다…

이제 퇴장해야 할 순간

죽음이 저만치 기다리고 있다.[8]

수잔나　배우의 놀이터,

아버지의 놀이터,

극장이 불타고 있다.

이제 무대에서 퇴장해야 할 때

아버지의 런던 생활

아버지의 모든 비밀을 품고 있는 저 곳

지금 불타 사라지고 있다

---

8) 〈맥베스〉, 5.5. 15-30.

한 세계가 사라지고 있다…

노쇠와 죽음만이 남았을 뿐.

아무 것도, 아무 것도 남지 않고…

재가 되어

엷은 공기 속으로

엷은 공기 속으로 사라진다.

No more, no more…

"벼락출세한 까마귀"[9]의 런던 퇴장

극장이 자기를 태워 작가에게 이별을 고하고 있다.

타오르는 불꽃은

작가의 퇴장을 기념하는

마지막 인사

다시는 돌아오지 말라 한다.

수잔나는 무대를 한 바퀴 돌며 춤을 추어 분위기를 바꾼다.

수잔나 그 어떤 개인적 기록도 남기지 않았던 당신.

편지 한 장도 우연한 메모 한 장도 남기지 않았다.

---

9) "Upstart Crow" 1592년 런던 연극계에 혜성처럼 등장한 셰익스피어를 일컬어 존 릴리(John Lily)는 이렇게 비아냥거렸다. 이 말 속에는 학벌이 없는 셰익스피어를 폄하하는 의미가 깔려있다.

왜 그랬을까?

뭔가가 두려워서?

영원한 미스터리

이 화재도 완벽한 공모자.

모두 다 태워 재로 만들었다.

당신의 작품은

오직

신의 자비로 살아남았다.

그 생명이 훗날 400년 이상 이어져 가도록!

(사이)

그리고

배우는 집으로 돌아왔다… 꼭 28년 만이다.

모두 사라지고 빈 무대. 앤 앞으로 나온다. 긴장한 모습이다.

앤   어떤 건 이제서야 온전히 이해가 돼.

(사이)

내 나이 곧 60. (사이) 세월이… 오래 살았어.

언제 윌이 날 떠났었지?

(사이)

사랑에 빠질 때 우리는 잠깐 행복했었다.

"우리는"은 아니었을지도 몰라. 나 혼자 행복했었겠지.

(쓴웃음)

어린 미성년자를 유혹해서 혼전 임신을 했다고 날 비난
하던 눈초리가 늘 내 뒤를 따라다녔어, 스물여섯 노처녀
의 필사적 결혼작전이라고도 했고. 하지만 사랑에 취한
내 귀에 그런 소리는 전혀 들리지 않았다.

(집을 둘러본다)

윌이 돌아올 줄만 알았지, 이 집 New Place에 처음 들어
올 때…

(사이)

런던에 아주 중요한 일이 있다고 했어. 그리곤 다시 가버
렸지.

(사이)

왜 난 안 붙잡았지?

아들 햄닛(Hamnet)[10] 은 겨우 열한 살…

그 애가 숨을 거둘 때

그때처럼 내 가슴이 쓰라리고 아픈 때가 없었어.

그 애가 가고 난 뒤 정말 난 사무치게 혼자였다…

세상이 텅 비었어…

세상이 텅 비었어.

그런데 이제 돌아온다고? 50이 다되어 다 늙어

이제서야 돌아온다고?

---

10) 셰익스피어 당시는 스펠링 표기가 유동적이었다. 보통 발음대로 적기도 했는
데 셰익스피어도 자신의 이름을 각각 다르게 쓰기도 했다. 햄닛은 햄넷으로 발
음할 수도 있다. 하지만 인물 Hamlet의 이름을 아들의 이름을 따서 지었을 것이
라는 추측으로 햄닛으로 표기한다.

돌아오겠다고?

(손과 팔을 심히 떠는 앤)

한여름 밤처럼 짧은 사랑, 사랑은 식고 너는 떠나가 버렸어,

딸 둘과 아들 하나를 내게 남겨 두고…

내 곁에 넌 없었고 나는 홀로였다.

(그녀의 하얀 긴 스카프만 어둠 속에)

〈3장〉

스트랫포드

뉴 플레이스[11] 식당

1613-14

식탁이 놓인 가족 식당. 앤과 주디스 굳은 표정으로 앉아 있다. 하녀가 시중을 들기 위해 뒤에 서 있다.

모두 말없이 기다린다. 이윽고 윌이 나타난다. 윌 오랫동안 비어 있던 아버지의 의자에 앉는다. 잠깐 가족을 일별한다. 하녀가 다가와 물을 따른다. 냉랭한 침묵이 흐르고 윌은 헛기침을

---

11) New Place: 스트랫포드에 세워진 가장 좋은 집. 셰익스피어는 이 집을 1597년에 60파운드로 구입하여 가족을 살게 했다. 5개의 박공이 달린 3층 저택에 방이 10개, 넓은 정원과 텃밭이 있으며 별채도 있는 큰 저택이었다. 셰익스피어의 가족은 이 저택에서 하인을 두고 풍족한 삶을 살았다.

하고는 유리컵을 집어 물을 마신다. 어색하다. 하녀는 음식을
각자의 접시 위에 담아준다. 주디스가 긴장한 채 포크를 들고
천천히 식사를 시작한다. 윌은 앤을 바라보려고 하지만 눈을
마주치지는 못한다. 앤은 움직이지 않는다. 윌은 그런 앤을 의
식하며 식사를 시작한다. 느릿느릿. 앤은 앞에 놓인 접시만 노
려보고 있다.

〈4장〉

월의 방

조용히 앉아 있는 윌. 책상 위에는 양피지 한 묶음, 잉크와 펜
이 있다.

윌   윌리엄 셰익스피어.
    (자신의 이름을 소리 내어 말하며 양피지 위에 쓴다. 현존하는
    유언장에 쓰인 그의 유명한 자필 서명이 무대 뒤 스크린 위에
    뜬다)
    연극이라는 허구의 세계… 아직도 날 매혹하나?
    (사이)
    지금 내가 어디에 있지? 고향 내 방에? 믿기지 않는다…
    런던…

제일 처음 쓴 시는 "비너스와 아도니스",
사우스햄턴(Southampton) 경에게 바쳤다. 나도 그때는 젊
었고 꿈에 부풀어 있었다. 마지막 희곡은 〈헨리 8세〉. 만
족스러운 작품은 아니었어. 존 플레처(John Fletcher)에게
맡겨둬도 충분히 쓸 만한 작품이었지.
내 마지막 작품이 내 무대 고별 극이 되어버렸다.
글로브극장이 그 공연으로 그렇게 불타 사라지다니. 아
이러니야.
(사이)
그건 거의 신탁이었다.
스트랫포드로 돌아가라는, 이제 앤에게 돌아가라는…
그보다 더 확실한 경고가 어디 있었겠어?
그래, 그래서… 난 돌아왔다.
이렇게 난 돌아와 지금 집에… 내 방에 앉아있다.
(침묵)
배우로 무대에 처음 섰을 때의 그 흥분
아직도 내 피 속에 돌고 있을까?
런던 쇼어디치(Shoreditch)에 '씨어터'[12] 극장이 있었지.
〈로미오와 줄리엣〉을 그 극장에서 처음 공연했다. 날 작가
의 자리에 확실히 앉혀준 공연이었어, 폭발적 인기였지.

---

12) 1576년 런던 북쪽에 처음 세워진 극장으로 이름은 'Theatre'였다. 1598년 버
   비지(Burbage) 형제는 이 극장을 헐어서 템스강 남쪽 서더크(Southwark)에 다시
   짓는데 이것이 글로브극장이다. 목재 건물이라 가능했다.

(사이)

그 '씨어터' 극장의 기둥과 지붕을 하나하나 떼어내던
밤. 아직도 기억에 생생해.

12월의 겨울 밤. 템스 강 얼음 바람에 뺨이 찢어질 것만
같았지. 극장을 해체했다! 버비지 형제와 우리는 건물
조각조각을 뗏목에 싣고 강을 건넜어. 그리고 강변 남쪽
언덕 서더크(Southwark)에 번듯이 다시 세웠어.
'글로브'극장을 우린 그렇게 만들었다.[13]

그 새 극장을 위해 1년에 3-4편은 족히 써내야했어. 낮
에는 무대에 섰고 밤에는 글을 썼지. 펜을 쥔 손가락이
다 부르텄어. 무섭게 글을 썼었다. 흐흐흐.

(오른손을 들어 쳐다본다. 사이)

내가 쓴 대사가 배우의 입에서 흘러나오고, 살아 있는
인물이 되어 울고 웃는다, 관객은 빠져들고 열광한다!
그처럼 가슴 뛰는 일이 또 어디 있지? 글로브극장, 인생
을 거기서 배우들과 다 보냈어.

그 극장은 이제 불타고 없다!

극장은 사라지고 나는 여기, 런던을 떠나 고향이란 곳에
이렇게 내려와 있다.

"Is this the promised end?"

---

13) 리차드 버비지와 커스버트 버비지 – 제임스 버비지의 두 아들. 형 커스버트는
글로브극장의 관리자(keeper)였고 동생 리차드는 당대 최고의 비극 배우였다.
셰익스피어의 햄릿, 리어왕, 오셀로, 리차드 3세 등의 연기로 유명하다. 극장은
1598년 12월 28일 밤 옮겨졌다.

(픽 웃음)

"이것이 약속된 종말인가?" "약속된 종말"

이건 켄트(Kent)의 대사다.

가장 확실한 "약속된 종말"… 그건 죽음이지.

(쓴 웃음)

리어 딸들… 막내 딸 코딜리어, … 그리고 거너릴과 리건.

윌은 '수잔나'라고 양피지 위에 쓴다. 무대 뒤 스크린 위에 Susanna Shakespeare라고 나타난다. 그는 Shakespeare에 줄을 그어 지우고 Hall이라고 위에 쓴다. Susanna Hall(수잔나 홀)이란 이름이 된다.

수잔나의 결혼. 딸은 스물넷. 사위 존 홀은 딸보다 8살이나 많았다.

(웃음)

앤이 나보다 8살 많은 것이 거꾸로 된 셈이었다. 앤과 나는 이때 공모자가 되었지. 암묵적 공모. 앤은 딸마저 어린 남자와 결혼시키고 싶지는 않았을 테니까.

(웃음)

앤은 스물여섯, 난 열여덟. 앤이 임신한 걸 알았을 때… 그냥 도망가고 싶은 생각뿐이었다. 내가 잠깐 몸 담았던 랑카셔도 떠올랐고, 런던도 생각했지. 만약 그랬다면? 앤은, 앤은 사생아를 낳고 천대와 무시 속에서 살아야

했을 거야.

(쓴웃음)

아니, 아니… 그때 당장은 아니었지만 결국 난 도망을 쳤던 거다. 어린 자식 셋을 남겨놓고 말이야… (쓴 웃음) 비겁했다. 우리 사랑은 그때 식어 버렸을까? 내가 스트랫포드를 떠났을 때. 흠, 사위가 수잔나를 버려두고 떠나는 그런 일은 없겠지. 수잔나가 아들이었다면 옥스퍼드로 보내 학자로 키웠을 거야. 그 애 눈이 날 딱 쳐다보면 내 속을 꿰뚫어보는 것 같거든. 그럴 때가 많아. 가끔은 그 눈을 피하게 돼…

(사이)

음, 주디스…

수잔나의 이름 아래에 Judith Shakespeare라고 쓴다. 스크린 위에 나타난다.

주디스. 스물아홉. 혼기를 놓친 딸. 알아. 결혼하기는 쉽지 않지.[14) 사실 결혼 안 하고 살아도 된다. (사이) 내 작품에 결혼 안 하고 산 여자가 있었나?… 젠장, 없군, 모두 결혼했어. 하지만 주디스는 그런 자유를 누려도 된다.

---

14) 이 시대 평균 수명은 45세 전후였다. 결혼적령기도 낮아지고 조혼이 성행했다. 주디스가 29세라는 건 당시로서 거의 결혼 불가능한 나이였을 것이다. 앤도 26세로 아주 늦은 결혼을 했다.

엘리자베스 여왕도 결혼 안 하고 잘 살았어. 애인은 있었지만. 내가 지켜줄 수 있다. 돈 걱정은 안 해도 돼.
(사이)
혼자 남은 걔가 사실 늘 마음에 걸려 있었어. 햄닛과 주디스… 쌍둥이 둘 중 하나는 죽고 하나는 살아남았으니 말이다. 걔 얼굴엔 그늘이 있어.

Hamnet Shakespeare(햄닛 셰익스피어)라고 쓴 후 조금 있다가 두 줄로 이름을 다 지운다. 스크린 위에 뜬다. 마지막으로 Anne Hathaway(앤 해서웨이)라고 쓴다. 그리고 Hathaway를 두 줄로 지우고 Shakespeare라고 쓴다. 윌은 두 손에 얼굴을 파묻는다.

으음… 앤… 앤…

이름 다섯 개가 나타나 있다. 이름들 점점 클로즈업되어 마치 관객의 얼굴에 부딪힐 것처럼 다가온다. 웅크린 윌의 몸을 삼켜버린다. 글자가 쪼개지고 부스러진다. 파편들이 눈처럼 떠다니며 쏟아져 내린다. 그러더니 하나의 큰 공 모양으로 뭉쳐진다. 점점 작아지며 소실점에서 어둠 속으로 사라진다. 교회 종소리 멀리서.

〈5장〉

햄닛의 무덤
교회 (성삼위일체 교회 Holy Trinity Church)

주디스, 모자를 쓰고 바구니를 들었다. 교회 바깥마당의 묘지에 들어선다. 햄닛의 무덤 쪽으로 다가간다. 여러 모양의 비석이 서 있는 교회 소속 공동묘지다. 종이 울린다. 한 십자가 앞에 월이 서 있는 것을 발견한다.

주디스
월　　주디스,

두 사람 한참 더 말이 없다.

주디스　(무덤에 다가간다) 올 때마다 이런 생각을 했어요. (사이) 딸인 내가 죽었더라면… 아들인 햄닛이 살고 말예요.
월　　(깜짝 놀란다) 누구 대신 누가 죽다니, 아니다.
주디스　그렇게 생각하죠?
월　　(딸의 눈을 피한다)
주디스　난 알아요. 햄닛이 죽었을 때부터 알고 있었다구요. 나를 쳐다보는 눈빛에 그런 마음이 다 담겨있었죠. 할아버지도, 할머니도, 엄마도.

월   그렇지 않아, 주디스.

주디스   아버지도 마찬가지였겠죠. 그렇죠?

월   아니다… 오히려 혼자 남은 네가 늘 마음에 걸려 있었어.

주디스   (의심스럽다)

월   넌 소중한 내 딸이야. 너희들이 크는 걸 많이 못 봤지만.

주디스   (햄닛의 무덤을 응시한다)

주디스   꿈을 많이 꿨어요. 내가 대신 죽고 햄닛이 살아나는 꿈을요. 그러면 엄마나 아버지가 반가워하며 걔를 품에 끌어안아요. 나는 무덤 속에 누워서 이걸 다 보고 느끼고 있고요. 그런데 난 일어설 수가 없어요. 모두의 눈길이 날 쏘아 보며 넌 그대로 관 속에 누워 있어 라고 말하는 거예요. 난 일어나려고 발버둥을 치는데 몸이 안 움직여지고 소리를 지르는데도 소리가 안 나오거든요… 그런 악몽을 꾸고 나면 한동안 마음이 내 마음이 아니죠. 몸도 아프고.

월

주디스   알고 싶은 게 있어요.

월   물을 때가 됐구나.

주디스   뭔 줄 알고요?

월   안다. 그 질문, 기다리고 있었던 건지도 몰라.

주디스   그럼 대답도 준비되어 있겠군요.

월   그래 물어보렴. 이제.

주디스   아버지가 우리를 떠난 이유. 집에 오면 꼭 이걸 묻고 싶었어요. 뭐죠?

(침묵)

월   나도 모른다. 이 좁은 스트랫포드를 벗어나고 싶었던 건 사실이다. 헛된 야망…

주디스   그런 정답 말고요, 우릴 버려야 했던 진짜 이유요.

월   너, 버린다는 말을 쓰는구나. 난 겨우 스무 살이었어.

주디스   스무 살. 어린 나이죠. 그래도 애가 셋이나 있는 아버지였고 남편이었잖아요. 어른처럼 굴었어야죠.

월   그 말은 맞다. 그러나 난 떠나야 했어.

주디스   그 떠나야 했던 이유. 우릴 버려두고 말예요. 그게 궁금한 거죠.

(침묵)

주디스   말해주세요.

월

주디스   우린 아버지 없이 자랐어요.

월

주디스   아버지가 있었다면 햄닛도 안 죽었을지도 몰라요.

월

주디스   햄닛이 죽을 때 얼마나 겁이 났는지… 그때 나도, 이 주디스도 사실은 죽었어요. 그 후 어떻게 살았는지 모르겠어요. 몸이 커지고 나이는 먹었지만 말예요. 늘 내가 살아남았다는 데 죄책감을 느껴야했어요. 할아버지 할머니 엄마 모두 슬퍼했지만 꼭 그게 날 탓하는 것만 같았거든요, 딸인 내가 죽어야 했는데…

월 주디스… 아니다.

주디스 아버지는 장례식에도 오지 않았죠. 엄마는 많이 기다렸어요.

주디스 아버지는… 그리고 수잔나만 좋아하죠, 똑똑한 수잔나와 난 늘 비교되었고.

월

주디스 난 결혼도 못하고…

월 주디스, 넌, 넌 결혼하지 않아도 좋다. 정말이다. 그냥 우린 같이 사는 거다.

주디스의 얼굴에 놀람이 스친다.

주디스 지금 뭐라고 하셨어요? 결혼 안 하고 같이 산다고요?

월 그래, 지금처럼. 우리 셋이 말이다.

주디스 난, 난, 그럼 런던에 갈래요, 거기서 아버지처럼 혼자 살고 싶어요. 여긴 날 원하는 남자는 없어요. 내가 원하는 남자도 없고요. 난 결혼 안 할 거예요.

월 그래, 결혼 안 하고도 살 수 있다.

주디스 정말이죠? 날 보내주세요.

월은 주디스의 손을 잡고 품에 안는다. 주디스 말없이 안긴다.

월   주디스… 햄닛…

VO   "인생이 겪어야하는 온갖 아픔, 온갖 번뇌를
      죽음은 잊게 한다.
      어리석은 우리 인생이 정녕 바라는 끝이지 –
      죽음– 그건 그저 자는 것일 뿐"[15]
      모든 것은 사라진다.
      이 지구도, 지구 위 삼라만상도
      마침내는 공기 속으로
      엷은 공기 속으로 녹아 스며들어가
      흔적도 없이 사라진다…
      우리 인생은
      꿈의 자료와 똑 같아
      잠으로 마무리된다.[16]

      종소리 약하게 먼 데서.

---

15) 〈햄릿〉, 3.1. 60-64.
16) 〈태풍〉, 4.1. 156-158.

[2막]

〈1장〉

1614

뉴 플레이스/에이번 강가

에이번 강가의 낡은 나무 벤치. 윌이 앉아 강을 바라보고 있다.
노을이 붉게 강을 물들이고 백조 몇 마리 아직 강에 떠 있다.
그는 피곤해 보인다.
집안에서는 수잔나와 주디스가 대화를 나누고 있다.

윌　　조용하다. 런던 템스 강변은 시끄럽기 그지없지. 곰이 으르렁 거리는 소리, 개 짖는 소리, 사람들이 고함치는 소리, 피비린내 나는 야만적 소리로 가득 차 있어. 에이번 강가, 여긴 조용하고 좋다.

수잔나　넌 모를 거야. 어릴 때 동네 아줌마들이 "너네 아버지 어디 갔어?" "언제 와?" "런던에서 뭐하냐?"고 날 늘 놀렸던 것. 더 어릴 땐 날 빤히 쳐다보며 실실 웃기도 했어. 난 기억해. 물론 이런 짓은 엄마에게는 감히 못했지.

주디스　나도 알거든. 뭐든지 너만 안다고 생각하지 마.

수잔나　그래? 너도 당했어?

주디스	한번은 참을 수 없어서 침을 뱉고 돌멩이를 집어 던졌어. 그 뒤론 날 못된 애라고 하더라.
수잔나	(웃음) 그래, 넌 찍힌 애였어, 맞아. 그런데 그 이유 때문인 줄은 몰랐네.
주디스	넌 날 보호해 주지 않았잖아? 어떤 땐 같이 날 놀렸지.
수잔나	(픽 웃는다) 너 못됐었어. 봐 아직도 날 언니라고 부르지도 않고. 너, 너, 너라고 하잖아.
주디스	(장난으로) 너, 너, 너, 수잔나.
수잔나	기집애, 철 좀 들어라.
윌	여기서 뭘 하고 있지? 그 늙은이. 뒤로 물러나야 할 때라고 느끼는 그 노인, 딸이 셋인 그 늙은이가 날 자꾸 괴롭히더군. 나도 어언간 그런 상황이 된다고 말야. 그래서 여기 이렇게 앉아 있지 않은가. 글쓰기를 그만두고 고향으로 돌아와 평범한 시골 늙은이가 되고 있다. 리어처럼 여자 셋이 내 옆에 있어. 한 사람은 마누라지만.
주디스	똑똑한 수잔나 언니, 혹시, 읽어봤어?
수잔나	한 두어 편. 어려운 말이 많아. 모두 다 이해한 건 아니야. 런던 사람들, 그런 어려운 말들을 정말 다 알아듣고 연극을 볼까?
주디스	얘기 좀 해봐,
수잔나	〈로미오와 줄리엣〉이라는 비극을 읽었어. 혼자 읽은 건 아니구, 남편이 읽어주면서 같이 읽었다고 해야 맞아. 아름다운 글이었어. 태어나서 처음 들어보는 언어. 주인공

둘이 어쩜 그렇게 한 눈에 반해 사랑을 하는지.

주디스 정말? 우리가 다 자기 극본 속에 들어 있다고 했는데.

수잔나 내게도 그런 말 한 적 있어. 그렇다면 이 사랑 얘기는 누구 얘기일까?

주디스 두 사람, 어떻게 돼? 결혼해?

수잔나 결혼은 결혼인데 비밀결혼을 해.

주디스 비밀결혼?

수잔나 두 집안이 서로 원수야, 그러니까.

주디스 원수인데 결혼을 한다고? 끝이 슬프겠다?

수잔나 둘은 죽어. 슬프지만 아름다워.

윌 다 잊은 줄 알았는데… 돌아와서 그 애초의 장면들과 다시 맞닥뜨렸다. 전혀 예기치 못했어. 여기 이 땅이 기억을 불러일으킨다. 앤과 처음 만났던 장소… 그 길을 난 다시 지나간다. 우리가 처음 키스했던 곳? 이 강가가 아니고 아든 숲속이었다. 한여름 밤이었어. 우리가 왜 숲 속에 있게 되었지? 내가 앤의 뒤를 쫓아갔던가? 모르겠다. 앤의 하얀 어깨가 달빛에 물들어 있었고, 그것만이 기억에 선명하다. 난 그 하얀 어깨에 키스했다.

수잔나 둘은 너무 어려. 줄리엣이 열네 살, 로미오가 열여섯 살. 철부지들이지. 혹시 우리 부모의 얘기가 녹아 들어간 건 아닐까 하고 생각했어. 둘이 보자마자 사랑에 빠지는데… 로미오는 애송이고, 줄리엣이 훨씬 성숙하고 적극적이거든. 엄마가 그러지 않았을까?

주디스　　엄마가…

수잔나　　로미오는 줄리엣의 미모에 정신이 더 팔려. 줄리엣보다 훨씬 미숙하다고 느꼈어. 줄리엣은 죽을지도 모르는 약을 마시거든. 그 용기 – 그 어린 줄리엣이 어떻게 그럴 수가 있지?

주디스　　독약을 마신다고?

수잔나　　젊은 엄마를 상상해봐. 엄만 자기가 원하는 남자를 찍어서 결혼할 수 있었어. 부모님은 이미 돌아가셨으니 결혼에 대해 간섭할 사람은 없었잖아. 그 미모에, 유산도 좀 있었고. 엄마 눈에 딱 들어온 사람, 자기보다 나이가 어려도 상관없다고 생각했을 거야.

주디스　　최고의 신붓감이었을 걸. 쇼터리(Shottery)와 스트랫포드에서. 나이는 꽤 있었지만.

수잔나　　(웃음) 너처럼?

주디스　　(웃음) 그래 나처럼. 뭐, 너도 일등 신붓감이었잖아.

수잔나　　그랬지, 부자 아버지, 유명인 아버지. 그래서 존 홀을 만난 거겠지. 그래도 엄만 너보다는 어렸어. (웃음). 아버지는 좀 조숙했을 거구. 또래 여자애들과는 말이 안 통했을 거야.

윌　　　　퍽(Puck)[17]이란 놈이 우리에게 장난을 쳤던 게 확실해. 퍽의 장난… 그놈이 내 눈 속에 사랑의 즙을 한 방울 떨어뜨린 게지. 불 같은 정염이 날 휩싸 안았어. 그 기억은

---

17) 〈한여름 밤의 꿈〉 아든 숲 속의 요정.

언제나 생생해. 그 성숙한 여인은 아름다웠고 난 어느 새 그녀의 품에 안겨 있었다.

주디스 엄마 미모에도 반했겠지. 로미오처럼.

수잔나 줄리엣이 로미오와 만나자마자 하는 말이 뭔지 아니?

주디스 결혼하자는 말?

수잔나 그래 바로 그거야. 엄마는 결혼이 급했을 거 아냐.

주디스 너 지금 나 비꼬는 거지?

수잔나 비꼬긴. 넌 결혼 안 할 거잖아.

월 그해 여름밤은 별똥별들이 많이 떨어졌어. 아마 그 혜성을 보러 아든 숲에 갔던 건지도 몰라.

수잔나 한 번 들어볼래? 내가 외우고 있어. 멋진 글이야.

"네 사랑이 명예롭고 진실하고
네가 결혼할 의사가 분명하다면,
내일 사람을 보내줘,
언제 어디서 식을 올릴 건지 말해줘
그럼 내가 너한테로 갈게.
내 모든 운을 너한테 맡기고
널 따라서 세상 끝까지 같이 갈 거야"[18]

이렇게 내일 당장 결혼하자고 해. 줄리엣이 먼저 말이야.

주디스 "세상 끝까지 따라 가겠다"고? (두 사람 시선이 마주친다. 웃

---

18) 〈로미오와 줄리엣〉, 2.2. 143-148.

음을 터뜨린다) 엄만 그렇게 한 셈이지. 오직 아버지를 기다리며 살았으니까.

수잔나 그렇지. 세상 끝까지 따라간다고 하곤 왜 런던으로 따라가지 않았을까? 그럼 우리도 시골 무지렁이 신세를 면했을 텐데. 그 사랑이 그렇게 식어버린 거지?… 너무 오래 떨어져 살았어.

주디스 28년.

수잔나 주디스, 혹시 런던에 애인이 있었을지도 몰라. 이건 내가 오랫동안 품어온 의심이다.

주디스 그렇게 긴 세월 동안… 없었다는 건 거짓말이겠지.

수잔나 연극계는 온통 남자 판이라고 해. 배우도 남자, 작가도 남자, 후원자들도 모두 남자 귀족. 하긴 남자 판이 아닌 곳이 없지, 세상이 모두 남자 건데.

주디스 여자 작가, 여자 배우 들어본 적이 없어.

수잔나 그런데… 주디스, 놀라지 마, 한 사람 있어.

주디스 (놀라서 믿기지 않는다) 뭐? 진짜?

수잔나 에밀리아.

주디스 에밀리아? 그게 누구야?

수잔나 에밀리아 라니어(Emilia Lanier)[19]. 책을 냈대. 시인이라고 했어. 대단하지 여자가 책을 냈다는 거.

---

19) 에밀리아 라니어(1569-1645)는 영국 최초의 여성 직업 시인이다. 시집 *Salve Deus Rex Judaeorum*을 출간했다. 그 책 속에 "Eve's Apology in Defence of Women"이라는 시가 있다. 최초의 Feminist 시인이라고 할 수 있고 셰익스피어의 소네트에 나오는 "Dark Lady"로 추정되기도 한다.

주디스   여자가 책을 쓰다니! 글을 배웠으니까 책을 썼겠지? 혹시 아버지의 애인이었을까?

수잔나   글을 아는 여성, 시를 쓰고 책까지 냈다면 런던의 유명인사겠지. 아버지가 모를 리가 없어. 극장에 와서 연극도 봤을 거야. 분명히.

주디스 갑자기 울음을 훅 터뜨린다.

수잔나   왜, 왜 그래? 주디스.

주디스   우리는 - 딸들은 문맹자로 남겨놓고…

수잔나   난 또 뭐라구, 그 여잔 난 여자야. 예외지. 우리완 달라. 다른 길은 없어, 여자들에겐. 몰라? 난 진작부터 알았어. 그래서 고분고분 결혼했던 거야.

주디스   우린 뭐지? 아버지가 영국 최고의 작가 시인 배우 윌리엄 셰익스피어! 그런데 우린 글도 모르는 무식한 시골 촌 무지랭이. 제 이름도 쓸 줄 모르고. 우리한테 너무했잖아! 학교도 남자만 갈 수 있고.

수잔나   그래 햄닛이 에드먼드 막내 삼촌과 학교 갈 때 나도 얼마나 부러웠는지. 간단해, 남자와 여자의 차이지. 넌 지금이라도 글을 배워. 결혼 따윈 하지 말고. 아버지가 그렇게 유명 작가가 되리라고 누가 상상이나 했겠어? 엄마도 몰랐을 거고. 마찬가지야. 너도 몰라 - 10년 후에 그 여자처럼 책을 내게 될지 누가 아니?

갑자기 시끄러운 새의 울음소리 같은 게 들린다. 윌 일어나서 강 아래쪽을 보더니 내려간다. 강변에 모여 있던 백조들이 놀라 푸드득 거리며 물속으로 들어가고 그 아래 쓰러져 몸을 떠는 백조 한 마리가 보인다. 멀리서 토마스 퀴니가 나타난다. 윌을 보고는 인사를 할까 말까 망설이다가 뭔가 심상찮은 일이 일어난 것 같아 가까이 다가간다.

토마스   아, 선생님, 무슨 일입니까?

        (백조는 쓰러져서 거센 호흡을 하며 신음 소리를 낸다)

        아, 이런-

윌   날개가 부러진 것 같은데.

토마스   늙은 백조군요. 날개도 부러졌지만.

        (두 사람 어쩌지 못하고 보고 있다. 백조, 마지막 소리를 내지르며 죽는다)

        죽었어요. 젠장. 재수 없어.

윌   (이 말에 놀라 토마스를 쳐다본다)

토마스   아, 셰익스피어 선생님, 인사가 늦었어요. 저. 토마스입니다.

윌   (잘 생각나지 않는다) 토마스?

토마스   네, 토마스 퀴니입니다. 양조장…

윌   아, 퀴니. 응, 양조장, 그렇지… 백조가 정말 죽었나?

토마스   네, 뭐, 아주 늙은 백조인데요, 죽을 때가 됐어요. 신경 쓰지 마세요.

윌

토마스 선생님?

윌 아, 음, 죽었어.

토마스 선생님?

윌 음, 그래, 리차드 퀴니,

토마스 괜찮으십니까?

윌 백조가… (정신이 든다) 토마스라 했지? 부친을 런던에서 한 번 만난 적이 있어.

토마스 그러셨군요. 선생님을 뵈니 아버지 생각이 납니다. 돌아가신 지 벌써 7년이 되었습니다.

윌 벌써?

(사이)

토마스 저도 런던에서 좀 살았습니다. 가업을 물려받았죠. 와인 양조장을 하고 있어요. 하이스트리트에 작은 가게도 열고 있고요. 지금 그리 가는 길입니다.

윌 와인 카페? 그렇군. 올해 몇 살이지?

토마스 올해 스물다섯이랍니다. 시골이 지낼 만하신가요? 앤 아주머니는 잘 계시죠?

윌 응. 우리 모두 잘 있네.

토마스 선생님 언제 우리 카페에 놀러 오십시오. 가장 좋은 와인 대접해 드리죠.

윌

토마스 곧 해가 지고 어두워 질 것 같군요. 노을이 흐려지는데요.

그럼 전 먼저 가겠습니다. 뵙게 돼서 영광입니다. 안녕히.

토마스 공손하게 목례하며 헤어진다. 한참 가다가 윌을 돌아보며 멈춰 선다.

토마스 (곁말) 저 분은 이제 부자에다 신분도 젠틀맨이 되었어. 내가 뭐 실례한 건 없겠지? 앤 아주머니를 아주머니라고 불렀는데, 뭐, 그럼 뭐라고 부르나? 마나님? 쳇! 한 동네에서 자랐고 집안이 서로 잘 아는 사이인데… 갑자기 마나님이라고 하려니 어색하잖아. 런던에서 꽤 유명세를 떨친다고 진작부터 소문이 났지.
아버지가 런던에 가셨을 때 두 분이 한번 만났었나 보군. 새로운 뉴스인데… 혹시 그때 저 분에게서 돈을 빌린 건 아닐 테지? 그때 30파운드[20] 빚이 있었는데… 돈을 빌리려고 만났던 건 아닐까? 모르겠다. 다 지난 옛날 일이야. 아무 말이 없는데 나서서 아는 척할 필욘 없지.

윌 (멀어지는 토마스를 돌아본다. 곁말로) 스물다섯? 그럼. 햄닛보다 네다섯 살 아래로군. 왜 꼭 햄닛의 나이를 기준으로하지? 내가?

토마스 퇴장할 때 주디스를 잠깐 일별한다. 주디스도 시선을

---

20) 당시 50파운드면 스트랫포드에서 꽤 좋은 집을 한 채 살 수 있는 돈이었다. 셰익스피어는 뉴플레이스를 120파운드에 구입했다.

느끼고 돌아본다.

토마스 눈이 마주치자 급히 사라진다.

〈2장〉

스트랫포드

존 홀의 병원이며 집 (Hall's Croft)

1614–1615

존 홀　스트랫포드 인근 땅이 거의 당신 아버지 땅이요. 이제 저 땅이 양들을 먹이는 초목지로 바뀌면[21] 수입은 더 늘어날 거야.

수잔나　런던이란 곳 또 극장이란 곳, 대단한가 봐요. 거기서 그렇게 부를 축적할 수 있었다는 게 믿기지 않아요.

존 홀　런던은 유럽 최고의 도시요. 인구도 가장 많고. 런던의 명물은 극장이지. 극장이 그렇게 많은 도시는 유럽에서 런던밖에 없어요. 템스강 주변은 극장이 10개가 넘어, 그러니 그 많은 무대를 채우려면 극작가와 배우가 필요하잖소! 극단도 아마 10개가 넘을 거야. 글로브극장은 곧 재

---

21) 15세기경부터 일어난 유럽의 초목지 운동으로 농지에 울타리를 쳐서 그 안에 양을 키우는 광범위한 운동이었다. 사유지화, 인클로저(Enclosure)운동이라고도 한다.

건될 거요. 장인은 계속 작품을 써야할지도 몰라. 모두 그
걸 원할 거야.

수잔나 아버진 은퇴했어요. 또 다시 런던으로 가지는 않을 거
예요.

존 홀 여기서 노년을 이상적으로 보내고 계시는 것 같소. 아직
기력도 그리 나쁘지는 않으시고. 재산도 상당하시지. 뭣
보다 사랑하는 딸인 당신과 가까이서 지내는 게 제일 좋
은 점인 것 같애요. 그래서 귀향하신 건 아니오?

수잔나 그럼요, 아버지 사랑이 특별하죠.

존 홀 당신을 코딜리어라 해도 될 듯해? 그런데 장모님과는 아
직도 좀 냉랭하신가요? 두 분은 잘 모르겠어.

수잔나 아직… 아버지는 노력하시는 것 같은데…

존 홀

수잔나 옛날에 할아버지가 시장 자리에서 물러나고 그 뒤 빚도
많이 지게 되었잖아요.

존 홀 알고 있소.

수잔나 갑작스럽게 사업이 그렇게 몰락했거든요.

존 홀 경제가 악화되니 고급 장갑 시장이 위축되어 버린 게지.
안타깝지만 말요.

수잔나 아들로서 그런 걸 만회하고 싶었을 거예요. 존 셰익스피
어는 망했지만 그 아들 윌리엄 셰익스피어는 런던에서
대성공을 거두고 고향에서도 큰 부자가 되었다. 이런 말
을 듣고 싶었을 거예요.

존 홀 젠틀맨 작위도 받으셨고, 장인은 이제 스트랫포드의 제일 가는 유지이고 어른이야. 자랑스러운 어른이지. 그런 분의 총애하는 큰 따님이 여기 계시네. (뺨에 살짝 키스한다. 웃음) 장인 돌아가시면 다 당신이 물려받을 거야. 집도 땅도 그리고 런던에 새로 산 집도 말이오.

수잔나 주디스도 있어요.

존 홀 아, 오해는 하지 마시오, 장인의 재산을 탐내는 건 아니오. 난 내 실력만으로도 충분히 명성을 얻고 있고 우린 아주 잘 살고 있잖소?

수잔나 환자들의 신뢰를 톡톡히 받고 있죠.

존 홀 알아줘서 고맙소. 하하, 그런데 궁금한 게 한 가지 있어.

수잔나

존 홀 런던의 집말이오. 귀향 직전에 그 집을 산 이유는 뭘까? 런던에 사실 때는 정작 집이 없이 하숙 생활하며 그리 오래 사셨는데 말이오. 궁금해. 당신도 궁금하지 않소?

수잔나 주디스와도 그 얘길 한 번 했어요. 정말 그 집을 왜 샀을까? 집으로 돌아오는 게 확실했는데 말이죠. 주디스는 지금 런던 그 집에 눈독들이고 있어요. 거기 가서 살고 싶어 해요.

존 홀 런던에? 결혼은 안 하고?

수잔나 결혼은 뭐, 이제 늦기도 했고. 혼자 살 거예요. 런던 가고 싶어 해요. 아버지처럼 런던에서 인생을 던지고 싶어 해요,

존 홀	여자 혼자 몸으로? 어려울 텐데. 런던 같은 대도시에서 여자 혼자 산다는 건 특히.
수잔나	부모님도 허락 안 하실 거예요. 주디스 저 혼자 희망사항이죠 뭐. 그나저나, 농지가 초목지가 되면 밀농사를 하던 농민들이 농사지을 땅을 잃게 되는 데 걱정이 돼요. 가난한 그들은 어디로 가야 하나?
존 홀	도시로 가서 싸구려 노동자로 전락하겠지. 도시 빈민층이 생기고 있는 이유가 그거요. 장인 혼자 사유지화 운동에 반대한다고 해서 그 큰 흐름을 막지는 못 할 거요.
수잔나	농민들의 반대도 거세어지고 있어요.
존 홀	너무 걱정하지 말아요. 관련된 사람이 장인뿐만 아니니. 지주 콤(Wiliam Comb)씨나 레플링엄(William Replingham)씨도 만만한 사람들이 아니야. 땅이 많은 사람들이 지세(tithes)를 포기하고 손해 볼 일은 절대 안 하지.[22]
수잔나	
존 홀	요즘은 뜸하시군.
수잔나	그분, 당신 눈엔 어떻게 보여요?
존 홀	강변을 자주 걷고 계시던데. 지금은 그냥 평범한 시골 노인? 마치 옛날부터 여기 스트랫포드에 죽 살아온 사람처럼 보이셔. 적응을 잘 하셨다구 할까요?

---

22) 레플링엄은 스트랫포드의 인클로저 운동의 중심에 있는 사람으로 셰익스피어는 자신의 토지가 사유화되어도 토지세를 안전하게 확보 받는 조건으로 그와 계약을 했다.

수잔나

존 홀 그래도 20년 이상이나 떠나 살았으니 고향이 낯설 수도 있어. 정을 다시 붙여야 할지도 몰라.

수잔나 평범한 시골 노인으로 보이는데… 실감이 나지 않아요. 런던 연극계를 손에 쥐고, 쓰는 작품마다 성공작이었던 극작가다, 글로브 극장의 주주였고, 여왕 앞에서도 또 제임스 왕 앞에서도 자주 공연을 했던 최고의 연극인이었는데 말예요!

존 홀 그래도 나이 들었는데 어떡하리오. 새로운 단어와 새로운 말을 만들어 내고 무운시(Blank Verse)도 창조하고 했지만 이제는 조용히…

수잔나 연세가 50이 넘었어요. 점점 약해지시는 것 같고… 무운시? 당신이 그런 것도 알아요?

존 홀 내가 장인의 애독자인 걸 모르시나요? 극장에서 연극으로 보기는 어렵지만 단행본이 출간되면 어떻게든 구해서 읽어본다오. 내 환자들이 런던에 갈 일이 있으면 부닥도 하고 말이오. 비극은 다 읽었지. 나도 의학서를 한 권 집필하려고 생각 중인데 문장을 쓰는 게 쉽지가 않아. 장인은 대단하십니다!

수잔나 놀랍군요! 나한테도 읽어줘야 해요.

존 홀 〈로미오와 줄리엣〉을 아주 맘에 들어 했잖소, 그럼 〈리어왕〉 실제로 읽어 볼까요?

수잔나 좋지요.

존 홀 그럽시다. 그럼 이번엔 〈리어왕〉 읽기.

수잔나 그분 이름엔 늘 최고의 수식어가 붙더군요. 당대 최고의 시인! 당대 최고의 극작가! 이런 화려한 타이틀로 수식되던 그분이, 강가에 멍하니 앉아 있는 지금의 저 시골 노인과 매치가 잘 되나요? 난 가끔 믿을 수가 없어요.

존 홀 흠.

수잔나 런던에서 몸과 마음, 특히 뇌가 바쁘게 살았던 분이… 갑자기 할 일 없는 촌로처럼 지내고 있어요, 같은 사람일까요?

존 홀 흠… 그래, 무슨 말인지 알겠소.

수잔나 그분이 부동산을 사들였던 것, 물론 런던에 있었을 땐 길버트 삼촌이 대행을 했지만요.

존 홀 당신 생각은 뭐요?

수잔나 돌아온 후 농장을 사기도 했는데… 당신은 재산 축적으로만 생각하지만… 그런 매수 행위는 내겐… 어떤 공허를 메꾸려는 행동같이 보여요. 그 농장이 뭐 그렇게 필요했을까요? 이미 많은 땅이 있는데 말예요.

존 홀

수잔나 극장을 향해 있던 그 열정, 작가라는 정체성, 그것이 사라진 그 텅 빔이 아버지 내면에 있을지도 몰라요. 그래서 그 텅 빔을 메꾸어 보려는 어떤 행동. 진짜 평범한 촌로가 되어보려는 어떤 노력, 아내와 딸들로부터의 거리감을 지워 보려는 안간힘. 내 눈엔 자꾸 그런 게 보이거든요. 그렇지 않을까요? 그렇게라도 자신의 존재를 확인해 보려는 그런 것 말예요. 그런데 어쩌면 그 발버둥이 공허한 것까지 다 알고 있거든요.

존 홀 (수잔나의 예리한 감성에 놀란다) 미처 생각지 못했어… 좋은 딸이오. 당신은. 그분은 복 받은 아버지고.

수잔나 아버지가 우리를 두고 떠난 이유를 조금은 알 수 있어요. 런던에서 그렇게 물렀던 이유도요. 발견한 재능을 포기하기란 어려운 일이죠.

〈3장〉

아든 숲 (Arden)
1615 여름

앤과 주디스가 숲에서 꽃을 따고 있다.

VO (노래로)
백리향 바람에 산들거리고
노란 앵초 제비꽃 피어있고
능소화가 드리워 있네.
사향장미 들장미로 뒤덮인 그 언덕
나는 알고 있어.

그곳에 티타냐가 자고 있을 걸.[23]

주디스 엄마, 여기 보라색 꽃, 백리향꽃.

아, 또 제비꽃도 있고- 둘이 비슷해서 구별이 안 돼.

앤 이쁘다. 이쪽에는 들장미가 아주 많이 피었어.

주디스 엄마가 제일 좋아하는 꽃이잖아요.

우리 정원에도 들장미는 많지.

오, 여긴 능소화.

두 사람 모자를 쓰고 꽃을 따는 모습이 꽃에 끌리는 나비와 같다. 새들도 지저귄다. 한참 꽃을 따고는 앤은 이윽고 그늘진 곳을 골라 천을 깔고 그 한쪽에 꺾은 꽃 더미를 두고 앉는다. 바구니를 열어 먹을 것을 꺼낸다.

앤 엘리자베스도 데리고 올걸 그랬다. 한참 못 봤어. 그 사이 또 많이 컸을 거다.

주디스 걘 수잔나를 많이 닮았어. 머리가 영리한 것도 말야. 알파벳을 벌써 다 배웠대요.

앤 그래? 부모가 모두 애 가르치는데 열심을 내는구나.

주디스 학교엔 못가도 걘 지 아빠한테 배우겠죠.

앤 너도 아버지에게 좀 배워보렴? 어때?

주디스 불편해. 그리고 집에 있지도 않고 늘 강가를 싸돌아다니

---

23) 〈한여름 밤의 꿈〉. 2.1. 249-253.

잖아.

앤   아버지가 와서 너 불편하니?

주디스   내가 묻고 싶은 말이야. 엄만? 엄마도 불편하지?

앤   그래, 젊을 때의 그 사람은 아니야.

주디스   난 아버지를 잘 몰라. 어린 시절 몇 번 보기는 했지만. 기
        억 속 그분은 늘 말이 없었고… 엄마를 두려워하는 것 같
        았어.

앤   날 두려워해? 왜? 뭣 땜에?

주디스   버려두고 갔으니까.

앤

주디스   엄마는 왜 아버지가 떠나갔다고 생각해?

앤   (갑작스런 질문에 놀란다. 손이 떨린다. 한 손으로 그걸 감추며
        누른다)

주디스   (손을 본다) 엄마…

        (사이)

        미안해, 엄마.

앤   괜찮다… 어린 나이에 갑자기 애 아빠가 됐으니 혼란에
        빠졌을 거라고 생각했어. 남자는 자기 몸으로 애를 낳지
        않으니 더 그랬겠지.

주디스   (앤의 손을 걱정스레 보며 신경 쓴다) 만일 아버지가 엄마랑
        결혼하는 걸 거부하고 그냥 숨어버리거나 도망을 갔다면
        어떻게 됐을까?

앤   그럴 가능성도 있었지. 그럴 경우 다시는 고향에 돌아오

지 않을 각오를 해야겠지만.

주디스 그럼 엄마는?

앤 네 언니는 사생아. 나는 미혼모. 동네 온갖 비난을 받아야했겠지. 얼굴도 들지 못하고 동네 바깥 한 쪽 구석에서 숨어 살아야 했을 거야. 마녀로 몰리지 않으면 다행이었을 거다.

주디스 엄만 재산이 좀 있었으니까 애는 혼자서도 키울 수는 있었겠지, 하지만 비난은 면치 못 했을 거야. 그렇지? 다른 동네로 가거나 도시로 가는 수도 있잖아. 익명으로 살 수 있는 곳. 도시로 가서 말야. 그럼 귀족 집안에 하녀로 들어가거나, 허드레 노동일을 해야 했을지도 몰라. 그 외에 다른 방법이 있었을까? 그럼 애는 어떻게 키우고?

앤 네 언니는 고아원에 맡겨야 했겠지? (웃음)

주디스 혹시 말야, 혹시… 엄만 애를 뗄 생각은 하지 않았어? 애를 떼고 런던으로 가버리는 것도 방법이잖아?

주디스를 바로 쳐다본다.

앤 그런 생각은 한 번도 안 했다. 그건 아주 위험한 생각이기도 하고, 둘의 목숨을 걸어야하지. 그리고 스물여섯에 첫아기를 가졌는데… 그게 내 마지막 찬스라고 생각했어. 결혼이 되건 안 되건 말야. 어렵게 결혼을 했지. 사실 네 아버지는 당장은 아니지만 도망을 간 거나 마찬가지야. 3년 후. 절묘한 타이밍을 잡아서 떠났지.

주디스 (한숨을 훅 토해낸다) 휴 ~ 엄마 그 세월을 어떻게 다 참고 살았어?

앤 왜 우리가 이런 얘기 하고 있지? 이렇게 좋은 날씨에?

하늘을 쳐다본다. 그녀의 눈에서 눈물 한 방울이 뺨을 타고 떨어진다. 그 눈물방울에 하늘이 비친다. 손은 여전히 떨리고 있다.

주디스 나 다 알아. 나 다 봤어. 아버지가 떠나가 버리는 것, 그 이후로 엄마가 혼자 외롭게 사는 것 – 다 봤어. 그분이 작년에 다시 돌아오는 것도 봤지. 그리고 그분도 외롭고 고독하다는 걸 봤어. 지금도 보고 있고.

앤

주디스 다시 떠나지는 않을 거야. 엄마 곁에서 늙어 갈 거야.

앤

주디스 런던에 샀다는 집 말이야… 엄마,

앤

주디스 그 집에… 내가 가서 살면 안 될까? 난 결혼 안 하고 내 마음대로 살고 싶어. 극장이란 곳에 가서 연극도 보고 싶고. 여자는 왜 이렇게 살아야 하지? 태어나서 할 일이란 게 결혼뿐인가? 여자도 영혼이 있고 자유를 누릴 권리가 있어!

앤 그런 생각 하지 말라고 글도 안 가르쳐 줬을 거야.

숲의 다른 쪽에 동네 처녀 마가렛 휠러와 메리가 나타난다. 앤
과 주디스가 인기척을 느껴 잠깐 그쪽으로 시선을 돌리지만
누구인지 확인은 하지 않는다. 마가렛과 메리도 앤과 주디스
를 보지 못한다. 마가렛은 20대 중반, 메리는 20대 초반이다.
두 여인은 즐거운 기분으로 꽃향기도 맡으며 노래를 부른다.
〈햄릿〉에서 오필리어가 부르는 노래다.

마가렛　(노래)

내일은 발렌타인 데이

새벽 일찍부터 그대 방 창 밑에 섰네

그대 발렌타인 되고 싶어서

그대는 일어나 옷을 입고 방문을 열어

날 받아 들이네

그 방 나올 때

난 더 이상 숫처녀가 아니야 [24]

메리　(노래)

세상에 이런 망측한 일이

사내놈들 원하면 지 맘대로 해

천벌을 받을 나쁜 놈들

그 여자애가 말했어

"날 쓰러뜨리기 전에 결혼 약속해놓고선" [25]

---

24) 〈햄릿〉, 4.5.47-54.

25) 〈햄릿〉, 4.5.58-63

두 처녀 깔깔거리며 장난스럽게 노래를 부르며 꽃을 따들고 지나간다.

[3막]

⟨1장⟩

초겨울 1615
에이번 강가

윌이 강가 벤치에 앉아 있다. 쓸쓸하고 추워 보인다. 늙었다.
해가 슬핏 지고 하늘이 서서히 붉게 물들어 간다. 백조 한두
마리가 가끔 퍼드덕 날갯짓을 한다.

윌　　백조가 물 위에 떠 있는 저 모습. 의젓하고 우아하다…
저렇게 죽음을 맞을 수 있다면 더 이상 바랄 게 없어.
(사이)
내 비극 속 인물들, 모두 비명에 죽었다. 비극이니 그럴
수밖에. (쓴웃음) 로미오가 가장 어린 나이였다. 그리고
햄릿, 젊은이들의 죽음, 맥베스, 시저, 오셀로는 중년의
죽음. 리어? 가장 나이가 많았어. 그렇게 늙었어도 죽기
전에는 제 어리석음을 깨우치고 죽어야 한다는 걸 말하
고 싶었지.
(사이)
나도… 죽기 전에 그 여인의 마음을 풀고… 이 무거운

마음의 짐 내려놓고 싶다.

주디스가 두툼한 담요를 가지고 나타나 윌의 뒤에서 어깨에 살포시 걸쳐준다.

윌　(어깨 위의 담요를 느끼며 딸에게 미소 짓는다) 코딜리어구나.

주디스　(웃음) 아버진 리어고?

윌　그래. 아니, 그렇게 어리석은 노인은 안 돼.

주디스　(옆에 앉는다) 추워요.

윌　춥다. 백조들도 떨고 있구나. 새들도 제 둥지를 찾아 어디론가 다 날아갔어.

주디스　그거 아세요? 백조는 한번 맺은 짝과는 평생을 함께 하고 새끼들도 함께 기른다는 걸.

윌

주디스　저 백조들이 다 여왕의 소유라는 게 사실인가요?

윌　벤 존슨은 날 에이번 강의 백조라고 부르곤 했지. 이 강에는 유난히 백조가 많구나.

주디스

윌　리어 그 노인은 코딜리어가 자기 곁에 있어줄 거라고 착각했다.

주디스　제가 코딜리어인가요?

윌　나도 그런 착각하고 있어. 넌 내 곁에 있을 거지?

주디스　엄마와 단둘이만 남게 될까봐 두려운 거죠?

월

주디스

월　　　네 엄만 틈을 주지 않는구나. 서릿발처럼 차가워.

주디스　 엄마 속마음은 안 그럴 거예요. 좀 더 기다려 보세요.

월　　　시간이 얼마 안 남았어.

　　　　　 침묵

주디스　 전 두 분과 함께 있을 거예요.

월　　　(안도하는 표정이다) 런던은 안 돼.

주디스　 3년만 살고 올게요.

월　　　함께 있겠다고 금방 말해놓고선…

주디스

월

주디스　 아버지, 청이 있어요.

월　　　런던은 안 된다고 말했어.

주디스　 아니, 글요. 글을 가르쳐주세요.

월　　　(작은 웃음)

주디스　 네?

월　　　글을 배워 뭐하려고?

주디스　 〈리어왕〉도 직접 읽어보고 싶어요. 아버지의 비극을 읽
　　　　　 어 보려고요, 책을 쓰고 싶어요. 그 여자 시인처럼요.

월　　　여자 시인이라니?

주디스 런던에서 책을 출판한 여자 시인. 아버지도 알죠?

월 아, 나도 소문은 들었어. 가십거리로 끝나고 말았지.

주디스 (놀란다) 그렇게 역사적인 일이 가십거리로 끝나다뇨?

월 그 책은 수많은 출판물 사이에서 곧 잊혀지고 말았을 거야.

주디스 역시 세상은 공평치 못하군요. 그 시집도 읽어보고 싶거든요. 그 여자 시인은 아버지 극장에 와서 연극을 봤을 거예요. 분명히.

월

주디스 아버지 연극에 나오는 남장한 여자들. 혹시 그 시인을 염두에 두고 쓰신 건 아닌가요? (이 말에 월은 당황한 기색이다) 그 여자들 할 말 하기 위해 남자 옷을 입은 거죠? 여자에겐 말할 기회도 주지 않고 귀 기울이지도 않으니까.

월 누가 그런 얘기를 해줬어?

주디스 글발 좋은 존 홀 박사가 얘기 해줬죠.

월

주디스 여자는 여자인 채로는 하고 싶은 말을 못하죠. 이런 세상 100년이 지나면 달라질까요?

월 포샤[26]에 대해 들었지, 그렇지?

주디스 네. 정말 기막힌 재판을 하지만 남장을 해야 그 말이 통하잖아요. 아무리 똑똑하고 재능이 있으면 뭘 해요? 여자

---

26) Portia 〈베니스의 상인〉의 여주인공. 남장으로 재판정에 나타나 샤일록을 재판하는 현명한 법관 노릇을 한다.

에게 그 재능이 저주가 되어버리지. 포샤처럼 남자 옷을 입어야 할 말 할 수 있는 이런 세상 언제나 바뀔까? 귀족 여자들도 다를 게 없어, 남들보다 풍족하고 화려하게 살 뿐, 시인이 되거나 배우가 되거나 그런 건 들어보지 못했어요. 그러니 그 최초의 여자 시인은 꼭 기억되고 널리 알려져야 해요.

윌

주디스   여왕이나 된다면 달라질까요? 하지만 엘리자베스 여왕 때도 여자 처지가 달라진 건 없었어.

윌   (미소 짓는다. 한 팔을 들어 주디스를 꼭 안는다) 그러니 넌 다르게 살아. 네가 원한대로 결혼은 하지 말고 100년을 앞질러 살아. 하지만 이 애비 곁에 꼭 붙어 있으렴.

주디스   아버지.

윌   (팔을 풀고 딸을 쳐다본다)

주디스

윌   너 코딜리어지?

주디스   코딜리어도 프랑스로 떠나가잖아요. 하지만 코딜리어처럼 남편을 따라가진 않을 거예요. 남자는 필요 없어요. 남자 따라 가는 게 아니고 간다면 나 혼자 갈 거예요.

윌   주디스.

주디스   아버지 런던에 보내 주세요.

윌

주디스   런던에 갈 거예요.

월   (벌떡 일어선다) 안 돼!

월과 주디스는 말없이 서로 노려본다. 주디스 아버지를 한참 노려보다가 몸을 돌려 화난 듯이 나가버린다. 월은 가만히 서 있다. 앙상한 나무 가지가 스산하다.

〈2장〉

1616 1월
뉴 플레이스 월의 방

쇠약해진 월. 책상에 앉아서 유언장을 쓰고 있다. 쓰는 내용이 뒷벽 전면에 뜬다. 월의 현존하는 자필 유서의 일부다. 방 한쪽에 유서감독인(overseer)인 변호사 프란시스 콜린스 (Francis Collins)가 멀찍이 앉아 있다.[27] 월은 자기만의 세계에 빠져 있다.

월   '종말'의 날이 이제 하루하루 셀 수 있을 정도다. 오늘이 될지 내일이 될지. 기력이 아직 남아 있을 때 정리해 놔

---

27) 콜린스는 셰익스피어의 부동산 취득에 도움을 준 변호사 친구이며 실제로 유 서를 받아 적고 후에 유서를 집행한 유서 감독인이다. 또 한 사람의 유서감독인 은 토마스 러셀(Thomas Russell)이다.

야 한다.

(한참 쓰다가 펜을 멈춘다)

런던 집. 그래 그 집. 블랙프라이어스(Blackfriars) 좋은 주택가에 산 집. 주디스가 가있고 싶어 했지만… 런던 그 복잡하고 험한 곳에 딸을 혼자 보내고 싶진 않았어. 애비 마음이지.

(사이)

그 집을 샀던 이유도 잊어버렸다. 런던에 자주 갈 줄 알았지. 내 연극동료들도 만나고 새 작품이 공연되면 가보리라 생각했어. 그리고… 그래, 그 한 사람. 그를 보기 위해서도 런던에 자주 가리라 생각했었지. 그런데 이렇게 스트랫포드에 콕 쳐박히게 될 줄은 몰랐다.

(사이)

런던 서더크. 성당 근처 실버스트리트에 살던 집이 기억나는군, 지저분하고 누추한 동네였지. 장사치들과 이민자들이 주로 모여 살던 동네였어. 몇 번 집을 옮기긴 했지만 그 동네를 벗어나진 못했다. 막내 동생 에드먼드도 가까이 살긴 했지만 너무 바빠서 걔를 챙겨줄 겨를이 없었어. 그게 미안해서 장례식은 제법 근사하게 치러주었지. 성구세주 교회[28]였다. 걘 배우가 되긴 했지만 운이 따르지 못했어.

(사이)

---

28) St. Saviour Church. 현재는 서더크 성당이다. 에드먼드는 여기에 묻혀있다.

내 셋집 주인은 프랑스 이민자였는데 그 집 2층 내 방
에는 침대 하나와 책상 하나만 덩그러니 있었다. 밤에는
촛불을 켜놓고 촛농이 뚝뚝 떨어지는 걸 보며 양피지에
글을 썼어. 내 손은 온통 잉크 물에 배어 있었고. 오른쪽
가운데 손가락은 불룩 튀어 나오고 못이 심하게 배겨있
었지.

(자기 손을 들어 본다)

깨끗한 주택지 동네에 집을 사서 편안하게 글을 쓸 수도
있었는데… (쓴웃음) 대신 난 스트랫포드에 이 집을 샀다.
치열하게 살았던 세월이었다. 어떤 땐 무대 위에서 즉석
에서 씬을 써서 배우들에게 던져주기도 했잖아. 리차드
버비지(Richard burbage)[29]는 그걸 단숨에 멋지게 읽어
내었지. 그때 난 정말 살아 있었다!

(침묵)

사실 〈헨리 8세〉를 쓸 때 난 이미 빈 쭉정이였어. 리어의
바보가 일러준 대로 텅 빈 코드피스(codpiece)[30]였다구.
창의력도 열정도 다 고갈된 상태였지. 불쌍한 텅 빈 그
림자, 걸어 다니는 그림자인간(walking shadow), 맥베스

---

29) 셰익스피어의 비극의 주인공을 도맡아 연기했던 당대 최고의 비극 배우.

30) 코드피스는 중세 남자들이 의복 위에 차던 성기 주머니였다. 여성의 브래지어
와 같은 기능을 했다. 노출되었기 때문에 귀족들은 화려한 수를 놓기도 하고 보
석을 달아 장식하기도 했다. 지나치게 사치로 흐르는 패션이 되자 법으로 금하
기도 했고 또 윗도리(doublet)를 길게 내려서 보이지 않게 하기도 했다. 딸들에
게 모든 재산을 다 주고 빈털터리가 된 리어를 바보(Fool)는 이렇게 부른다.

가 말한 대로 말이다. 난 그걸 알았어.

(한참 쓴다)

이 집은 수잔나에게 상속한다. 주디스는? … 결혼은 안할 거다… 내가 죽은 후, 이 집에서 앤이랑 같이 살면 된다. 수잔나가 엄마와 동생을 쫓아내진 않으리. 그래도 주디스에게 현금 300파운드를 남기련다… 채플레인에 있는 집도. 그리고 이 집안의 모든 접시도… 그 외 재산, 그리고 모든 부동산은 수잔나에게.

(쓴다)

수잔나도 아들이 없다… 직계는 끊어질지도 모른다.

(사이)

인간에겐 관 하나 묻을 넓이의 땅과, 몸을 가릴 옷 한벌- 그것이면 족할 것을… 의미 없는 재산이 이렇게 불어나 있다니.

(사이)

내 작품은 이미 만인의 것이 되었다. 연극을 사랑하는 모든 이들에게 바치는 내 선물이다. 언제까지 공연될지는 알 수 없다. 내 사후에 곧 잊혀 버릴 수도 있고… 아니면 시간을 뛰어넘어 살아남을 수도 있고…

(사이)

윌은 늙었다. 유언장을 쓰는데도 기력이 모자란다. 이윽고 펜을 놓자 변호사 콜린스가 다가와 유서를 훑어보고는 윌에게

서명을 하라는 제스처를 한다. 윌이 그를 올려다본다. 잉크를 다시 찍어 서명을 한다. 변호사 그걸 눈으로 확인하고 고개를 끄덕한다.

〈3장〉

뉴 플레이스
1616년 2월

세 모녀 침울하다. 긴장감 속에 있다.

수잔나 결혼 예식은 당장 올릴 수 없을 거야. 알지? 지금 사순절이 시작됐고 부활절까지는 기다려야 해.

주디스 4월 3일까지? 두 달이나? 그때까지 기다릴 수는 없어.

앤 (주디스의 배를 보며 살짝 터치한다. 불안하게) 주디스, 너 혹시?

주디스 아냐, 엄마, 그런 상상은 하지 마.

앤 그런데 왜 그리 빨리 식을 하려고 성화니?

수잔나 두 달만 기다리면 되잖아. 그럼 모든 사람의 축복을 받으며 식을 올릴 수 있어.

주디스 하루 빨리 어서 하자고, 기다릴 수 없다고…

수잔나 (픽 웃는다) 그러면 우스터 주교의 특별 허가를 받아야 할

걸. 식전에 교회 미팅에 2번은 꼭 출석해야 된다구. 그렇게 할 수 있어? 쉽지 않아. 그래도 꼭 해야겠니?

주디스

앤 딸아, 그런 게 아니라면서 꼭 이렇게 엄마 인생을 되풀이 해야겠니? 엄마도 우스터 주교의 특별 결혼허가서를 받아야했던 것. 알잖아.

주디스 엄마 미안해, 그냥 그렇게 하고 싶어. 빨리, 그렇게 결정… 내가 왜 이러는지 나도 모르겠어.

수잔나 (이 말에 웃음을 터트린다) 로미오와 줄리엣 놀이 하는 거야? 그 나이에? 제대로 걸렸나봐. 결혼 안 하고 런던에 가려고 할 때는 언제야?

주디스 수잔나, 가서 말 좀 해줄래?

수잔나 언니라고 해봐

주디스 (망설이다) 그래… 언니, 수잔나 언니.

수잔나 동생을 장난스레 노려보다가 앤의 눈 허가를 받고 윌의 방으로 간다.
한 층 위의 윌의 방. 그는 안락의자에 기운 없이 앉아 있다. 기력이 무척 약해졌다.

수잔나 아버지, 좀 어떠세요?

윌

수잔나 존을 오라고 할까요?

월	괜찮다.

수잔나 월의 상태를 살핀다. 월은 기운이 없다.

수잔나	아버지 좋은 소식이 있어요.
월	
수잔나	주디스가… 주디스가 결혼한답니다.
월	(믿기지 않는다) 뭐?
수잔나	
월	결혼이라니? 무슨 말이냐?
수잔나	네. 한대요.
월	주디스가? 갑자기… 상대가 누, 누구냐?
수잔나	아버지, 걔 나이가 서른하나예요. 주디스보다 나이 위인 싱글 남잔 이 스트랫포드에는 없어요. 모두 어린 남자 밖에.
월	그래서?
수잔나	토마스에요. 토마스 퀴니.
월	토마스? 리차드의 아들?
수잔나	네. 런던에 가서 일도 좀 배워왔고.
월	
수잔나	지금 하이 스트리트에.
월	안다.
수잔나	주디스는 스트랫포드에서 신부감 후보 1위였다나 봐요.

아버지가 부자로 소문났으니까요. 모두 돈을 보고 욕심을 냈겠죠. 하지만 뭐 주디스 나이가 있다 보니까…

월 아냐, 아냐, 아냐.

수잔나 아버지, 토마스는 우리가 어릴 때부터 아는 애고 그런 것 같지는 않아요. 주디스도 가벼운 애는 아니고.

월 믿을 수 없어. 아니야, 아니야, 수잔나, 오라고 해라.

수잔나 아버지, 걔는 겁먹고 있어요.

수잔나 나간다. 잠시 후 주디스 들어온다. 월 몸을 일으켜 곧추 앉는다. 주디스는 말없이 가만히 서 있다.

월

주디스

월 주디스.

주디스 아버지.

월 사실이냐?

주디스 네.

월 그 남자를 사랑하니?

주디스 (망설이다) 아마도요.

월

주디스

월 날 떠나겠구나.

침묵.

주디스   네, 언니처럼요. 아니, 엄마가 그 아버지를 떠난 것처럼요.

월   넌 결혼 안 해도 된다고 우리 얘기했어. 그렇지? 같이 산다구, 엄마랑, 나랑 셋이 말이다.

주디스   할 말이 없어요. 아버지.

월   허허 네가 코딜리어냐? 아니야, 넌 – 아니지? 그렇지? 다시 말해봐라.

주디스   제 속마음을 잘 표현할 수가 없군요.

월   넌 내 곁에 있겠다고 했다. 그렇지?

주디스   네, 알아요. 하지만.

월

주디스   아버지는 제가 런던에 가는 걸 원치 않았어요. 결혼밖에 이제 할 일이 없잖아요. 혹시 알아요? 토마스가 남편이 되면 날 런던에 보내줄지도. 혹은 같이 갈 수도 있겠죠. 아버지하고는 다를 겁니다.

월   딸아 꼭 그렇게.

주디스   (말을 막으며) 아버지, 걔는 열여덟 살이 아니에요. 스물일곱 살이죠.

월   (쓴웃음)

주디스   아버지는 날 코딜리어라고 여겼죠? 그 코딜리어가 아버지에게 뭐라고 말하던가요? 그렇게 사랑했던 딸도 이렇게 말하죠.

"내가 결혼을 한다면

내 남편은 내 사랑과 의무의 반을 가져가야 합니다.

아버지만을 사랑한다는 언니들처럼

저는 그런 결혼은 안 할 거예요."[31]

월   코딜리어는 쫓겨난 이후에 그렇게 말해. 넌 아냐, 난 널 쫓아내지 않았다. 넌 결혼 안 해도 된다. 주디스, 아니 코딜리어.

주디스   사순절 기간 동안이지만 식을 올릴 거예요. 물론 허락은 안 하시겠죠. 우리 결혼식이니까 허락은 필요 없어요.

월   (감정이 격해져서 벌떡 몸을 일으킨다) 넌, 넌 코딜리어가 아니다. 넌 애비를 속인 데스데모나야.

주디스   데스데모나도 그 아버지를 떠나서 남편 오셀로에게 갈 때, 그때 이렇게 말하지 않나요?

"내 어머니가 그 아버지를 사랑했지만

아버지보다는 남편에 대한 의무와 사랑으로 그 아버지를 떠났던 것처럼,

저도 아버지보다는 남편을 택합니다."[32]

월   아니야 – 안 돼, 넌… 넌… 넌 내 딸이 아니다…!

침묵. 주디스는 의자 위에 쓰러지는 월을 오랫동안 응시한다.

---

31) 〈리어왕〉, 1.1. 99-103.
32) 〈오셀로〉, 1.3. 185-189.

주디스 최선의 의도를 가지고 최악의 결과를 초래한 사람들이
우리가 처음이 아닙니다.[33]

앤이 들어온다. 주디스 조용히 나간다. 앤은 윌을 한참 바라본다.

앤 윌.

윌 (고개를 들고 앤을 쳐다본다. 의외로 앤이 들어와 있는 걸 보고
놀란다)

앤 잊어버렸어? 30여 년 전. 쟨 꼭 내 모습이야. 토마스, 토
마스가 저 앨 혼자 두고 떠나지 않기만을 바랄 뿐.

윌 내가 떠났던 건…

앤 그래, 떠났던 건, 떠났던 건, 그 이유가 뭔지 이제 난 상관
치 않아.

윌 난 다시 돌아왔소.

앤 죽을 날이 얼마 안 남아서 돌아왔겠지, 살 날이 많았을
땐 떠나갔고. 당신은 오래 오래 살아 저 딸을 잘 지켜봐-

앤은 팔과 손을 떨기 시작한다. 점차 떨림이 심해진다. 윌의
시선이 그 손에 닿자 앤은 나가버린다. 윌은 간신히 다음의 말
을 내뱉는다. 힘들게 거의 들리지 않게.

윌 몸이 많이 상했어… 으음. (신음)

---

33) 〈리어왕〉, 5.3. 3-4.

(사이)

내 작품에 결혼 생활을 잘 하는 부부는… 없다. 맥베스
부부? 권력의 욕망에 뜻이 맞았을 뿐. 실제로 오랫동안
같이 산다는 건 전혀 다른 이야기지. 감정적으로 친밀하
면서 몸과 마음을 서로에게 잘 적응시키는 진짜 부부 말
이야. 그런 걸 우리는 "행복한 결혼 생활"이라 부르지.
로미오와 줄리엣이 죽지 않고 같이 살았다면, 오래 오래
말이야, 그런 건 상상할 수가 없다. 그들이 사랑한 시간
은 고작 8일 간 – 그리고 죽었다. 내가 그린 부부는 모두
단절되고 고립된 부부다. 거너릴과 올바니 부부가 바로
떠오르는군. 거너릴은 사랑에 목이 말랐는데 남편 올바
니는 메마른 목석이었어. 오셀로와 데스데모나. 레온티
즈와 허마이오니[34]도 그런 부부다. 행복한 부부는… 없
다. 오, 앤… 주디스… 내 코딜리어…

〈4장〉

1616년 3월 15일
달밤

노란 반달이 떠있고 지바퀴 새 울음소리가 나지막이 불안하게

---

34) 〈겨울 이야기〉 주인공 부부. 질투로 인해 파국을 맞는다.

들린다.

앤   이 밤에 새가 울고 있네,
    너도 혼자구나.
    짝을 잃었어.
    (새 소리에 귀를 기울인다)
    정든 님이 그리워서 우는 거니?
    나도 너처럼 울어나 볼까?
    무정세월
    님은 돌아와도
    내 님이 아니로구나.
    어제 청춘이
    오늘 백발이다.
    (새 소리 귀를 기울여 다가간다)
    이리 온.
    이리 오렴.
    내가 안아 줄게.

살그머니 가서 새를 손에 안는다. 떨리는 손이다. 새는 어딘가
에 상처를 입었는지 날지 못하고 띄엄띄엄 발자국을 떼다가
비틀거리며 쓰러진다. 앤이 가만히 손바닥 위에 새를 품는다.
새는 몸을 떨며 앤을 본다. 조그맣게 울음소리를 낸다.

그래 그래,

어디, 다쳤어?

왜 그리 울었니?

배가 고팠어?

짝이 그리워 울었니?

(새를 쓰다듬으며)

몸을 떨고 있네.

불쌍해라.

너 아니?

(새를 쓰다듬으며)

내 딸이 꼭 30년 전 내 신세야,

저 가엾은 처녀도 30년 전 내 신세야.

새 울음소리에 여자의 진통 소리가 오버랩 된다. 앤은 놀라서 몸이 굳어진다.

뒤에서 마가렛이 출산 진통을 겪고 있다. 옆에 그의 어머니 조운과 산파가 있다. 메리는 옆에서 울고만 있다. 이 장면은 반투명 막 뒤에서 진행되며 그림자로만 보이고 소리로만 들린다. 앤은 무대 앞에 홀로 서서 이 소리를 다 듣고 있다.

조운   딸아, 딸아, 이걸 어떡해, (산파에게) 어서 좀, 어서요,

산파   아직 안 돼, 마가렛, 얘야, 어서 이름을 말해, 누구 자식인지, 그래야 내가 도울 수 있단다.

마가렛 진통으로 괴로워하며 소리를 눌러 삼킨다.

조운   에고 이러다가 딸 죽이겠네, 산파, 빨리, 손 좀 써 봐. 그
           게 지금 뭐가 중요하다고.
산파   마가렛, 정신 차리고… 그래야 애기도 너도 무사해, 어서
           애 아비 이름을 말해라. 네가 말을 해야 나도 널 도와줄
           수 있어. 그렇게 지시를 받았단 말이다. 나도 어쩔 수 없
           어. 불쌍한 것 – 메리, 넌 알고 있지? 네가 말해라.
메리   난 몰라요, 난 몰라요. (운다)

마가렛 정신을 잃었다 깼다 한다. 진통이 막바지에 이른다.

조운   더 이상 못 보겠어. 내가 애기를 받아야겠어. 딸을 죽일
           셈이야, 어찌 그리 모질게.
산파   안 돼, 안 돼, 저리 비켜.

조운이 손을 쓰려 하지만 산파가 막아선다. 두 여자가 옥신각
신한다.

앤   불쌍한 것. 왜 말을 안 해, 네가 무슨 죄를 졌다고. 온 동
           네 지켜보고 있었는데 쉬쉬하고 우리만 몰랐던 거야. 이
           제 난 알아. 그 애 애비는 토마스, 토마스 퀴니. 내 딸 주
           디스의 남편이다. 토마스는 저 불쌍한 마가렛과 결혼해

야 했다. 저 애를 미혼모로 아기를 사생아로 만들 참이
야? 불쌍한 마가렛. 왜 말을 하지 않니? 말해라, 토마스,
토마스 쿼니라고!
(다시 여자들의 말소리, 울부짖는 산모의 소리가 들린다.)
안 돼, 저런, 저런, 그렇다고 산파가 가만있다니. 누가 그
런 지시를 했지? 빨리 빨리 좀 도와줘. 안전하게 아기를
받아줘. 허락된다면 내가 내가 키울게. 불쌍한 것들…
오, 하나님 자비를! 마가렛, 제발, 제발 무사하기를!

마가렛   (외마디 소리) 토마스, 토마스… 쿼니.

모든 소리가 없어지고, 순간 정적이 감돈다. 이어 산모의 고통
에 찬 소리가 찢어질 듯 들린다. 아기가 태어난 것 같다. 그러
나 아기의 울음소리는 들리지 않는다.
갑자기 조운의 울음소리가 터진다. 앤 바닥에 웅크리며 주저
앉는다.
음악이 이제 모든 소리를 다 감싸 안아 흐른다.
오필리어의 노래 소리(2.4)가 마가렛의 목소리로 음악 사이로
들린다.

VO   "내일은 발렌타인 데이
　　　　새벽 일찍부터 그대 방 창 밑에 섰네
　　　　그대 발렌타인 되고 싶어서
　　　　그대는 일어나 옷을 입고 방문을 열어

날 받아들이네

그 방 나올 때

난 더 이상 숫처녀가 아니야

날 쓰러뜨리기 전에 결혼 약속해 놓고선"

앤은 새를 품은 채 고개를 푹 숙인다. 새가 가냘프게 운다. 수
잔나 들어온다.

수잔나 어머니, 아기도 마가렛도…

앤

수잔나 주디스 결혼 후 겨우 한 달 만에 이런 일이 일어나다니
요.[35] 왜? 왜? 믿을 수가 없군요. 토마스는 이 모두를 알
고 있었겠죠? 주디스도 알았을까요? 열 달 동안이나 입
을 다물고 있다니. 불쌍한 마가렛. 토마스가 결혼 언질을
줬던 걸까요? 입막음 돈이라도 줬던 걸까요? 불러오는
배를 보고 얼마나 애가 탔을까요?

앤 내 딸도 마가렛도 둘 다 불쌍하구나.

수잔나 토마스가 결혼하는 걸 보고 얼마나 낙담했을까요? 결혼
식을 서둘렀던 이유가 이것이었다니. 마가렛과의 결혼을
피하는 게 목적이었어요. 특별허가서도 못 받고 교회에
서 파문을 당하면서까지 주디스와 빨리 식을 올릴 필요
가 있었군요. 그게 이유였어요. 그리고 아버지의 돈 - 주

---

35) 2월 10일 주디스 결혼, 3월 15일 마가렛 사망.

디스가 상속받을 재산이 탐났던 걸까요? 사랑은? 사랑은 어디로 숨었을까?

앤 우리 모두가 마가렛을 죽인 셈이다.

〈5장〉

1616년 3월 25일
월의 죽음 한 달 전부터 죽음까지
월의 방

월은 유언장을 고쳐 쓰고 있다. 겨우 한 자 한 자 아주 힘들게 쓴다. 옆에 술병과 잔이 하나 놓여있다.

월 이제 죽음이 바로 저기 문지방에 서 있다.
난 기꺼이 그 미지의 길을 갈 것이다.
아무도 거부할 수 없고 아무도 다시 돌아 올 수 없는 길.
발버둥치지 않고 의젓하게
잠자듯이… 이 마지막을 받아들이련다.

술을 한 잔 마신다. 독약을 마신 듯 얼굴이 찡그려진다. 한숨을 내뱉는다. 그리고 쓴다.

VO   (윌의 목소리로. 하지만 죽어가는 윌의 목소리와는 대조적으로 뚜렷이)

내 유언장에서 그놈 토마스의 이름을 모두 삭제한다. 그놈이 혹시 받게 될 수도 있는 상속분을 모두 수정한다. 내 직계 손자가 아니면 절대 그 어떤 것도 손 댈 수 없게. 내 재산은 수잔나의 아들, 또 그 아들에게로 내려갈 것이다.

사이.

월   주디스에 대한 실망을 이렇게라도 표현할 수밖에 없다. 이 유언장을 공개하는 날 딸은 알게 될 것이다. 이 아비의 쓰라린 마음을.

VO   애초에 생각했던 300파운드는 반으로 줄인다. 채플레인에 있는 주디스 명의의 부동산(집)은 수잔나에게 양도할 경우 50파운드를 받을 수 있다. 그리고 150파운드는 주디스의 아들이 3년 이상 살아 있을 경우에 해당 이자를 받을 수 있다.

월은 힘들게 계속 유언장을 수정할 때 앤이 무대 앞 한쪽에 등장한다. 두 사람은 거리를 두고 떨어져 각자 독백을 뱉어내지만 이건 또 다른 종류의 대화일 수도 있다.

앤 　토마스 사건은 우리 모두에게 큰 자국을 남겼다. 윌은 충
　　격으로 갑자기 더 늙어 버렸다. 시간이 없다. 죽기 전에
　　할 말이 있어.

VO　이 집을 포함한 거의 모든 재산은 수잔나에게 상속한다.
　　앤을 언급하지 않아도 그녀는 아내로서 1/3을 가질 권리
　　가 있다. 그러니 이것만 밝혀놓아도 충분하리라.

윌 　우리 집의 두 번째 좋은 침대를 앤에게 준다.

　　무대 뒤 벽에 현존하는 이 부분의 자필 유언이 뜬다.

앤 　뭐라구? 두 번째로 좋은 침대? 그 침대를 내게 준다는데,
　　이게 무슨 말이지? 우린 각자 자기 침대가 있어. 설마 우
　　리가 결혼 초기에 같이 썼던 그 침대를 말하는 건 아니겠
　　지? 헨리 스트리트의 집에 있던? 도대체 이게 무슨 말이
　　야? 정신이 흐려지나 보다. 안 돼. 우리가 이렇게 작별할
　　수는 없어.

윌 　두 번째로 좋은 침대…

앤 　어떤 건 이제서야 확실히 이해가 돼. 당신 마음은 여기서
　　런던이 먼 것만큼이나 멀었어. 왜 내가 런던으로 가지 않
　　았지? 걸어서 발이 부르트고 찢어진다 해도 갈 수 있었잖
　　아. 오라는 말은 한 번도 한 적이 없었지만 말이다. 아 우
　　리 사랑은 한여름 밤처럼 짧았어,

윌   더 이상 머리가 돌아가지 않는다. 기억도 흐려진다. 눈이
아프다. 잘 보이지가 않아. 코딜리어가 이 사실을 알고 있
었는지 상상하기도 싫다. 역겹다. 애비를 이렇게 저버리
다니. 넌 데스데모나보다 더 나쁜 년이다.

(술을 한 모금 더 마신다)

오, 오, 주디스, 불쌍한 것. 그렇게 앞당겨 빨리 결혼식을
감행해야 했던 그 속마음이 오죽했을까? 왜 이 애비에게
말 못했지?…

(사이)

(쓰디쓴 웃음을 터트린다)

내 인생 5막에서 일어난 최고의 반전이야!

이 5막의 사건이 1막의 사건과 겹치는 중복 구성(plot)이
로구나.

그러니 더 기발하고 더 기가 막힌다!

위에 계신 분 역시 몇 수 위시로구나.

내 인생 드라마를 이렇게 완벽한 구성으로 마무리해 주
시다니.

마지막은 신의 터치에 의해서 만들어진다.

햄릿이 말했지, "우리의 종말을 빚는 건 신이다"[36]

아, 아, 난 "운명의 노리개"[37] !

앤   늘 당신을 생각했어.

---

36) 〈햄릿〉, 5.2. 10.
37) 〈로미오와 줄리엣〉, 3.1. 138.

윌	(고개를 든다)
앤	런던에 있을 당신 애인도 매일 생각했어.
윌	앤, 애인이라고 했어?… 당신이 최초의 최고의 애인이었다는 걸 먼저 말해 두고 싶어. 그 후 무수한 애인이 있었지만 말이오.
앤	
윌	에밀리아도 그 중 한 사람. 딸이 이 이름을 말할 때 깜짝 놀랐지. 그리고 사우스햄턴 백작도 그 중에 있어. 앤, 그는 남자야. 내 마음에 특별한 자리를 차지한 남자. 내 첫 시를 그에게 바쳤지. 우리 극단의 후원자 귀족나리. 나보다는 한참 어렸어. 세상의 풍파를 모르는 순수하고 고결한 아름다운 젊은이였다.

그의 부탁으로 〈리차드 2세〉를 공연하던 밤. 에섹스 백작의 무모한 반란 음모에 우리 극단이 엮였었지. 에섹스는 자신이 볼링브록이라고 생각하고 그 연극을 우리가 공연하도록 했던 거지… 에섹스는 처형당했어. 그리고 에섹스를 처형한 여왕도 곧 죽었다.[38] 사우스햄턴 백작은… 간신히 석방되었어. 천운이었지. 아 그때 내가 얼마나 마음을 졸였던고. 그의 목숨을 살려달라고 간절히 기도했어 간절히. (생각에 잠긴다) 이런 건 왜 아직 기억이 |

---

38) 1601년 〈리차드 Ⅱ〉 공연. 리차드 2세는 영국 최초로 왕위 찬탈을 당해 죽은 왕이다. 볼링브록은 헨리 4세가 된다. 에섹스 백작은 쿠데타를 일으켰으나 실패. 1603년 엘리자베스 여왕이 죽고 제임스 왕이 등극한다.

또렷하지? 시간이 좀 남았을까?

술병에 다가가던 손이 멈추고 급히 눈을 더듬으며 감싸 쥔다.

앤　지금 무슨 소릴 하는 거지? 남자를 사랑했다는 말이야?
　　그런 헛소릴 지껄일 시간은 없어. 이제 곧 죽음이 닥쳐,
　　죽기 전에, 윌, 정신 차려.
윌　… 눈이… 눈이… 앞이 보이지 않아.

눈의 고통이 점점 심해지는 것 같다. 엎드려 고통스러워한다.
두 사람의 대화는 어느 사이 가깝게 엉킨다. 두 사람의 몸은
무대 양쪽에 멀리 떨어져 있다. 무대 전체는 어둡고 오직 두
사람 위에만 빛이 떨어진다.

윌　알아… 앤, 당신이 날 기다리고 있었다는 걸. 하지만 난
　　런던에, 런던에 있어야했어. 대신 돈을 보냈지…
앤　우리에게 풍족한 삶을 준 건 맞아. 그렇다고 그게 전부가
　　아니야. 그렇다고 해서 모든 게 용서되는 게 아냐, 가슴
　　저미던 그 외로움은 오직 내 몫이었어… 런던으로 왜 우
　　릴 데리고 가지 않았지? 왜 우릴 여기 이 시골에 버려두
　　었냐고! 말해봐
윌　외로움이란 말… 무척 낯설게 들리는군. 극장과 무대를
　　잠시라도 내 생각 밖으로 몰아낸 적이 없었거든. 물론 글

쓰기에 고독은 꼭 필요하지. 이렇게 말하면 당신은 이해할 수 있을까? 내가 혼자 살지 않았다면 내가 창조한 그 언어들은 태어나지 못했을 거라구.

눈의 통증으로 괴로워한다. 앤은 그를 담담히 쳐다본다.

앤 뻔뻔하군. 작가를 이해하지 못할 거라고 날 무시하는군? 런던에서 출세했다고… 그게 너 혼자 잘나서 그렇게 된 거 같애? 내가 그 떠남을 묵인하지 않았다면? 내가 보내주지 않았다면 그게 가능했겠어? 재능이 있건 없건 넌 여기서 내 남편으로, 세 아이의 아비로 살았어야 했어. 네 빈 자리를 누가 메꿨지? 연극이 대체 뭐야? 네가 사랑한 그 연극 – 그건 온통 거짓말, 사랑도 우정도 다 꾸며낸 거야. 왕도 귀족도 진짜가 아냐. 그 따위 네 연극이 없었다고 세상이 더 답답하고 더 불행했을까?
세상은 원래 그렇게 생겨먹었어. 그런 네 연극을 위해서 난 뭐였고, 우리 가족은 뭐였지? 사람들이 당신을 천재라고 하던데? 네가 천재가 되는 동안 난 외로움과 사투를 벌였지, 아들이 죽는 것도 혼자 지켜봐야했어, 딸들은 아비 없이 놀림을 당하며 컸어. 우리는 이렇게 살았어, 당신 없이.

윌 앤, 당신은 여전히 어찌할 수 없는 근엄해 빠진 청교도군.

앤 그래 넌 그 썩어빠진 가톨릭이야. 겉으론 프로테스탄트

인 척하고 있지만

월 좁혀지지 않는 틈 -

앤 그 틈이 건널 수 없는 강이 됐어.

월 앤, 최초의 그 사랑을 기억해 봐. 그런 사랑은 오직 우리만이 할 수 있었어.

앤 그 사랑도 가짜였어, 그러니 넌 떠났고.

월 아냐, 그 사랑은 신이 주신 선물이었어. 내가 글을 쓸 수 있었던 것도 그 사랑을 경험했기 때문이었다고 믿고 있어. 지금은 식어버린 사랑이라 해도 우리가 그런 사랑을 했다는 것- 그 새겨진 기억이 우리에게 살아갈 힘을 주었던 거고. 나도 이건 뒤늦게 이제야 깨우쳤어.

앤

월 그래서 당신도 날 마음에 품고 기다릴 수 있었던 거지. 안 그렇소?

앤 그런 말이 날 위로할 거라곤 생각지 말아. 넌 내겐 영영 철들지 않는 어린 소년, 철부지 어린애야.

월 (쓴웃음) 하지만 난 죽어가고 있어, 앤, 날 봐.

앤 누군들 아니겠어? 우리 모두는 죽어.

월 (아픈 눈을 잡고 괴로워한다)

앤 내 삶은 살만한 가치가 있었을까? 넌 나와 바꿔서 살 수 있냐고 묻고 싶어.

앤 쪽 서서히 어두워지고 월에게만 빛이 남는다. 어느 순간 앤

은 보이지 않고 마치 온 세상에 혼자 남은 듯, 윌은 혼자다. 떠
듬떠듬 윌은 어렵게 다음을 고백한다. 두 눈의 통증을 무릅쓰고.

윌   내가… 내가 당신을 떠났던 건, 아니 당신에게 더 일찍
돌아오지 못했던 건, 아니 내가 런던에 계속 머물러야 했
던 건… 그 아름다운 젊은이 때문이었다고 하면 앤, 당신
은 날 더 미워하겠지. 그는 날 일개 배우로, 그리고 극본
쓰는 연극쟁이로 대수롭지 않게 여겼지만, 그는 내게 특
별했어. 늘 도달할 수 없는 거리가 존재했지만 난 늘 그
를 흠모했지. 그를 그리워하며 소네트를 썼어…
(사이)
그가 글로브 극장에 나타나 내 연극을 봐줄 땐 그를 위
해 죽어도 좋다고 생각한 적이 한두 번이 아니었어.
(자조의 웃음. 웃음소리 점차 높아진다)
아 그때, 극장이 불탈 때… 거기서, 극장 안에서 죽었어
야 했어…

윌은 말을 마치자 허수아비처럼 털썩 주저앉는다.
사우스햄턴 백작이 업스테이지에 나타난다. 푸른 눈, 붉은 빛
을 띤 갈색 머리가 어깨 위까지 출렁인다. 수려한 미남. 20대
초반의 모습. 손에 두루마리를 쥐고 있다. 윌이 헌정한 시다.
무대를 한 바퀴 가로지르며 윌에게 다가간다. 가만히 그를 쳐
다본다. 윌은 놀라 얼굴을 들고 그와 눈이 마주친다. 젊은이는

미소 짓는다. 윌은 일어나 그의 손에 쥐어진 두루마리를 본다.
백작이 그것을 펴서 보여준다.
무대 뒤에 소네트 29의 후반부가 나타난다.

VO   그대를 생각하노라면
나는
첫 새벽 어두운 대지 위로 날아올라
천국의 문 앞에서 노래 부르는 종달새.
그대 사랑이 날 부요케 해
(아아)
그 누가 내 운명을 부러워하지 않으리!

윌은 그를 잠시 포옹한다. 그 포옹을 풀고 백작이 다시 오던
길로 사라질 때, 앤이 1막의 검은 의상을 입고 백작이 등퇴장
한 그 길을 그대로 즈려밟고 다시 나타난다. 마지막 즈음에 두
사람이 살짝 스친다. 앤은 눈길을 백작으로부터 거두어 윌을
잠시 응시한다. 그에게 다가간다. 적절한 시기에 이들의 모습
이 영상으로 뒷벽에 나타난다.
윌이 비틀거리며 걷다가 넘어진다. 다시 일어나려고 애쓴다.
불안하게 걸으며 앤을 잡으려 하는 것도 같지만 방향을 잘 모
른다. 앞이 보이지 않는다. 부부의 단절과 충돌이 표현되고 드
러나는 동작들이 나타난다. 이런 동작들은 마지막에 가서 더
욱더 심화된다.

월   여기가 내 여로의 끝.[39]

눈먼 배우가 여기 서 있다.

퇴장하라는 큐가 떨어졌는데

그런데 난 길을 잃었다…

인간의 가치는 그 죽음이 드러내준다[40]고 했는데,

(사이)

세상은 극장이고

무대 위

우리 인간은 등장과 퇴장을 따르는

배우에 지나지 않아[41]

수잔나와 주디스가 1막의 검은 의상으로 손에 들풀과 들꽃을 들고 등장한다. 이제 세 여인은 월을 둘러싸고 리어의 딸들처럼 보이다가 점차 맥베스의 세 마녀로 옮아간다. 1막에서처럼 세 여인은 춤과 움직임을 대사와 곁들인다. 마치 장님놀이를 하는 것처럼 눈먼 월은 세 여인의 뒤를 더듬거리며 따라가 잡으려고 하는 것 같다. 수잔나와 주디스는 꽃과 풀을 월의 머리와 옷에 꽂아준다. 무대 위에도 꽃과 풀이 떨어진다. 무대 위 모습이 계속 클로즈 업 되며 영상으로 나타난다.

---

39) 〈오셀로〉, 5.2. 265.
40) 〈헨리 4세〉 2부, 2.2. 47.
41) 〈좋으실 대로〉, 2.7. 139-142.

수잔나 불쌍한 배우. 우리 인생은 걸어 다니는 그림자,[42]

주디스 세상은 무대

우리 모두는 등장과 퇴장을 따르는

배우일 뿐. 우리는 꼭두각시.[43]

앤 그렇게 가면 안 돼

우린 할 말이 더 있어

내 속에 있는 못 다한 말

다 들어주고 가야지

내 말, 말, 말…

수잔나 말.

주디스 못다한 말.

윌 아 – 아– 악 – 애 – ㄴ

월의 정신은 혼란스럽고 마지막 생명줄이 촛불처럼 거의 다 타들어간다. 비틀비틀 걸음을 옮기는데 마치 벌판의 리어처럼 보인다. 알지 못할 소리도 지르며 옷을 찢으려 하거나 머리를 흔들며 꽃을 떨어트린다.

주디스 엄마처럼 살고 싶지는 않았는데…

(사이, 허탈한 웃음)

허허허

---

42) 〈맥베스〉, 5.5. 24.

43) 〈좋으실 대로〉, 2.7. 139-142.

　　　　그런데 엄마의 복사판

　　　　마가렛이 나 대신 죽었나요?

　　　　내 꿈을 다 무덤으로 가지고 가 파묻었어요.

　　　　혼자 런던으로 가지 못한 걸 후회하고 있어요.

　　　　혼자, 혼자, 혼자

　　　　여자 혼자라는 것에 세상은 겁을 집어먹게 하죠

　　　　세상은 그렇게 해도

　　　　아버진 날 보내줬어야 했어요.

　　　　내 운명을 시험해 볼 수 있게

수잔나　　배가 오고 있어.

　　　　강을 건너야 해. 우리가 모르는 곳

　　　　누구도 다시 돌아오지 못하는 곳

주디스　　태어날 때 우리가 우는 건

　　　　바보들의 무대에 등장했기 때문에

　　　　그래서 슬퍼서 우는 거라고 - 그렇지?[44]

수잔나　　북소리다 북소리가 다가온다.

　　　　강 안개가 짙어진다.

　　　　바람이 분다.

주디스　　바람이 분다.

　　　　아버지

　　　　아버지

월　　　으 - 으- 윽 -불어라, 불어라 바람아, 불어 뺨을 찢어

---

44) 〈리어왕〉, 4.6. 180-81.

라.[45]

주디스   강 안개가 흩어지고.

비바람 사이로 해가 비치네.

수잔나 나쁘고도 좋은 이상한 날

나쁘고도 좋은 이상한 날[46]

주디스   나쁘고도 좋은 이상한 날

나쁘고도 좋은 이상한 날

앤   육신은 사라진다.

숨결처럼 공기 속으로 스며 사라진다.

어디로 가는 거지? 어디로 가는 거지?

모든 근심의 실타래를 푸는 잠속으로

상처를 씻어 낫게 해주는 향유 같은 잠.[47]

주디스   죽음의 모조품인 솜털 같은 잠.

윌   sleep, no more…

주디스   잠

수잔나   잠, 죽음 같은.

윌 고꾸라진다. 세 여자, 윌의 몸을 둘러싼다. 그의 죽음을 확
인한다. 앤이 혼자 따로 선다.

---

45) 〈리어왕〉, 3.2. 55.
46) 〈맥베스〉, 1.3. 36.
47) 〈맥베스〉, 2.2. 40-42.

주디스 아버지, 아버지
당신은 떠나고
난 떠나지 못하고

수잔나 안녕히…
배가 곧 떠난다.
조명을 꺼라
막을 내려

음악 잦아들며 수잔나 무대 앞으로 나온다. 앤은 어둠 속에 꼿
꼿이 서 있다. 주디스는 윌 옆에 몸을 굽히고 애도한다.

수잔나 호흡이 멈췄다. 죽음은 이렇게 찾아왔다. 4월 23일.
시, 희곡, 그리고 유언장이 그가 남긴 전부.
강박적일 정도로 아무 것도 남기지 않았다.
마치 이 세상에서 자신의 존재를 감추려고나 했듯이
아무 것도 남아 있지 않다.
심지어는 자필 원고마저도 사라져 남아 있지 않다.
왜?
무엇이 두려웠을까?
신교가 득세한 세상에서
가톨릭이란 걸 숨기기 위해?
그것이 이유일까?

이런 연유로 후세 사람들은 의혹에 휩싸인다.

프란시스 베이컨? 크리스토퍼 말로? 옥스퍼드 백작?

거론되는 이름들이

논쟁거리로 떠올라 많은 사람들을 괴롭히게 될 거다.

진짜 작가가 아닐지도 모른다는 의혹이 그의 존재감을

더 증폭시키고

우리를 더 매혹시킨다.

혹시 이것마저 그분이 미리 생각해둔 건 아닐까?

나는 딸 수잔나이고 나와 우리 가족이

그분이 생존했던 가장 분명한 증거.

그분은 현존하는 37편의 희곡을 쓴 당사자였다고

난 믿는다.

주디스 꼭 1년 후 아들을 낳았다. 이름을 셰익스피어 퀴니라고

지었다.

하지만 그 아긴 6개월밖에 살지 못했다…

난 또 아들 둘을 더 낳았다

그런데

스무 살 즈음 둘 다 모두 역병으로 죽고 말았다.

아

난 말을 잃어 버렸다

집 밖에 나가지도 않았다.

남편이었던가? 토마스 퀴니라는 남자는 혼자 어디론가

가버려

종적을 감추었다. 그는 돌아오지 않았고 어디서 어떻게
죽었는지
아무도 모른다.
누군가 런던에서 봤다고 했는데
왜 그는 어디론가 갈 수 있었지?
마음대로
혼자서도

수잔나   어머니는 아버지 타계 7년 후 돌아가셨고, 그 해 최초의
셰익스피어 전집
폴리오(Folio)가 출판되었지만 보지 못했다.
나 수잔나 홀은 66세로 죽었고
주디스는 나보다는 좀 더 살았지만
처절한 고독 속에서 삶을 마쳤다.
아버지는 성삼위일체교회에 묻혔고 어머니는 아버지 옆
에 묻혔다.
나와 남편도 아버지 옆에 묻혔다.
어린 햄닛의 무덤은 오래 전에 사라졌고
주디스의 무덤도
교회 밖 마당 어딘가에 묻혔는데
무덤의 자취는 곧 없어져
먼지가 되었다…
모든 것은 먼지가 되었다…

앤   어리석은 우리 인생이 정녕 바라는 건 –

모든 근심의 실타래를 풀어주고

상처를 씻어 낫게 해주는 향유 같은 잠.

여로의

끝

이다.

세 여인의 움직임 제의적으로 변해간다. 점점 잦아들며 동결
된다. 그 몸 위, 빛이 한번 순간 밝아진 후 어두워진다. 연극이
끝난다.

The Promised End

A play by Jihoon Yi

Translated by Jihoon Yi
and Daren Jonescu

This play is selected by
ARKO 2020 Play Contest

Characters

Anne Hathaway

Susanna

Judith

Margaret Wheeler

Joan Wheeler

Mary

Midwife

Will Shakespeare

John Hall

Thomas Quiney

Henry Wriothesley, 3rd Earl of Southampton

Francis Collins, solicitor

A maid

A bird

Anne, wife of William Shakespeare, is 58 years old. Their first daughter Susanna is 31. Susanna is married to John Hall and they have a daughter Elizabeth, 5 years old. Judith, the second daughter, is 29.

Notes on the text

* The appearance of characters' names with no dialogue indicates silence. These are the spaces that actors must fill with their emotions, eyes, facial responses, bodily gestures, and so on.

* The quotations(" ") are from the original texts.

[Act 1]

⟨Scene 1⟩

Bare stage. Three women in black dresses.

Anne Hathaway wears an ankle-length coat and holds a white chiffon scarf. She is old but has graceful beauty. Susanna wears a long sleeveless dress with a wide, glossy enamel belt around her waist. Judith wears a see-through blouse and a long skirt with a hat or scarf on her head, and is barefoot.

They move or dance slowly or swiftly to percussion music. Their movements express their feelings and their relationships.

A man intrudes upon the three women. He is Will. He wears a 17th century style doublet and a white ruffle around his neck. He reaches out to catch the women but is somehow rejected; they are repeatedly intertwined but push one another away in dance forms. Will writes poems instantly on pieces of paper and throws them into the air. The white papers fly and fall to the stage like snow. This is seen on the screen behind.

Susanna   *(catching one paper flying around, reads)*

"The lunatic, the lover, and the poet

Are of imagination all compact.

The poet's eye, in a fine frenzy rolling,

Doth glace from heaven to earth, from earth to

heaven."

Judith   *(catching one paper flying around, reads)*

"And as imagination bodies forth

The forms of things unknown, the poet's pen

Turns to shape, and gives to aery nothing

A local habitation and a name."

Judith   *(throwing her paper and catching another, reads)*

"Life's but a walking shadow, a poor player

That struts and frets his hour upon the stage,

And then is heard no more. It is a tale

Told by an idiot, full of sound and fury

Signifying nothing."

Anne   *(picking up a fallen paper, reads)*

"Men are April when they woo,

December when they wed."

"A young man married is a man that's marr'd."

Susanna   *(throwing her paper and catching another, reads)*

"How many ages hence

Shall this our lofty scene be acted over

In states unborn and accents yet unknown."

Will   *(tossing papers)*

Look at me

Look at me

Look at me

Hold up a mirror up to the world

Life is a play

The stage mirrors our lives.

Anne   *(catching a paper abruptly falling down in front of her face, reads)*

"Let still the woman take

An elder than herself."

All secret marriages end in tragedy.

Judith   *(picking up a paper on stage, reads)*

"but

If thou dost break her virgin knot before

All sanctimonious ceremonies may

With full and holy rite be minister'd,

No sweet aspersion shall the heavens let fall

To make this contract grow; but barren hate,

Sour-ey'd disdain, and discord, shall bestrew

The union of your bed with weeds so loathly

That you shall hate it both therefore take heed,

As Hymen's lamps shall light you."

Susanna   *(catching a paper, reads)*

The blessed marriage must have

Father's approval

Father's blessing

And a great deal of dowry.

Will   World is theatre; theatre is world.

The Globe Theatre is a globe, the earth, the world…

A theatre is within a theatre

The theatre within a theatre, within a theatre…

within…

Susanna   Fog is getting thick,

Can't see at all,

"Where shall we three meet again?"

Judith   "In thunder, in lightning, or in rain?"

Anne   *(unwillingly)* When shall we meet again?

Judith   "Tomorrow, tomorrow, tomorrow."

Susanna   Whom shall we meet again?

Judith   A poet, an actor, a lunatic.

Anne   A cold-hearted lover, a boy, an old man.

Susanna   The young boy left his girl,

She waited and waited and waited

She became an old lady alone.

Judith   Time flows even during a tempest or an earthquake

Whither has gone the beauty of the woman he once

loved?

It dried up like a dewdrop.

But her daughters grew up and turned out as beautiful

and mature as she.

Will   All secret marriages end in tragedy.

All of a sudden we see the burning Globe Theatre upstage. The canopy and pillars fall down in fire. Anne and Judith are shocked and leave. Will, aghast, stands taken aback. He is frozen by this inconceivable sight. The scene continues to Scene 2.

⟨Scene 2⟩

London

1613

Before the Globe

Will is still standing shocked.

Will   Your time is over.

"You are a poor player

That struts and frets your hour upon the stage,"

But now you have to exit

Your time is over.

(pause)

The Globe is gone

enclosing all the tales

"told by an idiot, full of sound and fury,

signifying nothing."

I have "crept in this petty pace from day to day

To the last syllable of recorded time…"

To this last moment, to my journey's end

There's no tomorrow, no tomorrow, no tomorrow…

Now the land unknown awaits me.

Susanna   The playground of the actors

The playground of my father,

Is burning

Time to exit the stage

Time to exit from his London life.

The secrets of my father

All burning down with the Theatre,

A world disappearing.

Only aging and death remain.

Everything

Into thin air

Into thin air

Everything comes to smoke and ashes

No more, no more…

Exit the upstart crow

Exit from London

The Globe is saying a last goodbye to him,

It is whispering into his ears, "Don't come back,"

By burning its own flesh and bones.

Susanna moves and turns around the stage. The atmosphere changes.

Susanna   You never left any personal writings or records.

Not a single letter, no accidental notes.

Why is this?

Afraid of something? It is a mystery.

The fire was a perfect accomplice

Everything reduced to ashes,

Your works alone survived, by God's benevolence.

(pause)

And

The old actor

Came back home… after 28 years.

Will and Susanna exit. Anne appears. She is nervous.

Anne   Some matters are understood late.

(pause)

I am soon 60. The years… I have lived too long. When did he leave me? I have forgotten.

(pause)

We were happy when we loved. It may not have been "we". Perhaps I alone was happy. *(bitter smile)* Suspicious eyes have followed me, asking if by any chance I had seduced him. I was much older than he. They thought an old girl tempted an immature young boy. They thought it was my cunning marriage strategy. But I didn't care about the gossip. I truly fell in love with him.

(She looks around the house.)

I believed he would come with us here to New Place when we moved in.

(pause)

He said he had business to do in London and left.

(pause)

Why didn't I hold him back? Why couldn't I?

(pause)

Our son Hamnet was just eleven.

As he died... I suffered alone, without you.

So alone on the earth after the boy was gone...

Empty world... empty me...

You... what?... you will come back? Now?

Come back home now?

(Her left arm and hand start shaking painfully.)

A brief love was like a midsummer night;

Love cooled, you went away,

Two daughters and a son were left to me...

You were not here with me

I have been alone all this time.

In darkness, her white scarf is dimly seen.

⟨Scene 3⟩

Stratford

The family dinning room, New Place

1613–1614

Anne and Judith in their day dresses sit at a large dining table. They look stiff and uncomfortable, waiting in silence. Will enters. He sits at the head of the table, which has been vacant for a long time. He eyes his family briefly. A maid approaches and pours water in his cup. Still cold silence.

Will coughs awkwardly and drinks water. The maid puts food on their plates.

Judith picks up her fork and tries to eat. Will would like to make eye contact with Anne, but he dares not. Anne sits still. Conscious of this, Will begins to dine very slowly, while Anne just stares at her plate.

⟨Scene 4⟩

Will's room, upstairs

Night

Will is sitting quietly in candlelight. On his desk a pack of paper, a quill, and a pot of ink.

Will   *(as he writes)* William Shakespeare.

The well-known signature of his will is shown on the screen.

The illusory theatrical world...

does it still fascinate me?

(pause)

Where am I now? I cannot believe it, although it is real.

My first published poem was "Venus and Adonis," dedicated to Lord Southampton. I was young and had dreams. *Henry XIII* was my last play. A bit disappointing. I should have let John Fletcher do the job alone. That might have been better. My last play became truly the last one. The Globe has gone with the play forever. How fitting.

(pause)

It was an oracle telling me to go home, go back to

Anne. There could be no clearer direction than that. So, at last, I have returned and here I sit in my room in Stratford. It is real.

(Silence)

My excitement and enthusiasm when I first acted on the stage, where is it? Is that heat still circulating in my blood? It was at Curtain that *Romeo and Juliet* premiered. That performance was certainly the one that confirmed me as a playwright. It was a great crowd-pleaser.

(giggles)

The memory is vivid. The winter night we dismantled the building of The Theatre.[1] We tore down the pillars and timbers. A frozen December night. The icy wind on our cheeks, the materials ferried over the Thames, and Burbage rebuilding it as The Globe on Southwark, the bank side. I wrote two or three plays a year, did I not? Sometimes four. I acted by day and wrote by night. I wrote and wrote. My fingers swollen and sore from holding the quill. Very painful, and yet I was entirely alive. I was mad.

---

1) The first theatre built (1576) in England for the sole purpose of presenting plays.

(He grins and looks at his right hand.)

The words spoken out of the mouths of the actors, the words that bring life to men and women who fully breathe, laugh, and cry. The words lead the audience to shout with joy! tremble with tears!

The Globe... I spent my life in it. But then it was gone. It is no more, and I am here in my room, far from London.

"Is this the promised end?"

(a bitter smile)

The promised end. Kent spoke the words as he witnessed Lear's last breath. The most certain "promised end" is... death.

(a bitter smile)

Lear and his daughters. Cordelia, Goneril, and Regan.

Will writes Susanna Shakespeare on the paper. It appears on the screen. He soon crosses out Shakespeare with two horizontal lines and writes Hall on it.

Susanna Hall is now on the screen.

Susanna's marriage. She was twenty-four and John Hall eight years older. *(grinning)* Bridegroom older than bride – a reversal of our case. There was an implied understanding between us. Anne wished her daughter never to marry a younger man.

(laughs quietly)

I was just eighteen and she twenty-six. When I learned she was with child, I, I longed to run away. To Lancashire? to London?

If I had done... she would have been an unmarried mother of a bastard and lived a life of disgrace and contempt.

(a self-rebuking chuckle)

I ran away at any rate... not then but three years on. After another birth, the twins. I was a coward. When was it? Was it when I left Stratford, that our love turned cold?

(pause)

John will never do such a deed as I. If Susanna had been a son? I might have raised her as a scholar. She would have gone to Oxford. Sometimes I feel uneasy when she looks at me directly. I try to avoid her eyes somehow.

(pause)

Mm... Judith...

He writes Judith Shakespeare below Susanna Hall. It is shown on the screen.

Judith... twenty-nine. Too late to marry? Perhaps a rare chance to meet eligible men above her age. But marriage is not an obligation, she is free not to marry. She may live with us. Us? *(cynical smile)* Anne and me.

(pause)

Is there a significant woman living alone in my plays? Hm... No... Not a blessed one. All married or about to be so. Judith, however, may enjoy the freedom not to marry. Elizabeth our Queen never married, though she had a great many suitors. I can support my daughter. She never has to worry about money.

(pause)

In truth I always think of Judith, the surviving twin. One dead, one alive. I see a dark shadow on her face.

He writes Hamnet Shakespeare and crosses out the name with two horizontal lines. It is seen on the screen. Lastly, he writes Anne

Hathaway and crosses out Hathaway and writes Shakespeare on it.
He looks at the name and buries his face in his two hands.

Anne... Anne...

Five names are on the screen. Slowly the names grow bigger, as
though moving closer to the audience. The oversized names begin
to break apart into pieces that grow to overwhelming size and then
disappear.

The church bell rings from a distance.

⟨Scene 5⟩

Hamnet's grave
Holy Trinity Church
1613–14

Judith enters the graveyard. She wears a hat and holds a basket.
A number of tombstones. She approaches Hamnet's tomb. The bell
tolls. She sees Will at the tomb.

Judith

Will   Judith.

(Silence)

Judith   *(walks close to the tomb)* Whenever I come here, I think of my death. I should have died instead of Hamnet. Hamnet is a son and should live.

Will   *(surprised)* You die in his stead? No, no, no.

Judith   You thought so, too, didn't you?

Will   *(avoids her eyes)*

Judith   I know. I've known that since he died. I could read their eyes' saying so. Grandfather, Grandmother, and Mother too.

Will   No, Judith.

Judith   Your eyes are saying the same thing.

Will   No... I think of you always because you are the remaining one...

Judith   *(doubts)*

Will   You are my precious daughter, although I could not be with you as you grew up.

Judith   *(looking at the tomb)* I have dreamt. In my dreams I die and Hamnet comes back to life. Then you and Mother run and embrace him. You three are all very happy. Lying in the coffin, I see and feel this. I try to move and rise up, but I can't. And the eyes of all the people stare at me, and they shout at me to lie still in my coffin. I desperately try to rise up and up, but I fail. I try to yell, but my voice makes no sound. The nightmare repeats. Nightmares...made me ill. My mind and body are very ill.

Will	
Judith	I want to know one thing.
Will	This moment, I knew it would come.
Judith	What? What do you think it is?
Will	I knew. The question. I have been awaiting it.
Judith	Then your answer is ready.
Will	Yes. Now you ask.
Judith	The reason you left your family. I truly want to know it.

(silence)

Will	I... don't know. I merely wished to escape from Stratford. This small country town. And my vain ambitions.
Judith	That's a ready-made answer. I don't want that sort. I want the real reason you had to abandon us.
Will	Did you say "abandon"? I was but twenty.
Judith	Only 20. Yes, you were young. But you were a

	father of three children. and you were a husband. You had to behave as an adult.
Will	You are right. But I had to go.
Judith	The very reason you had to go. I mean the reason why, why you abandoned us. I want to hear it from you.

(Silence)

Judith	Tell me.
Will	
Judith	We grew up without a father.
Will	
Judith	If you had been with us, Hamnet might not have died.
Will	
Judith	I was so afraid when he died. I thought I was dead along with him. I don't know how I've lived until now, though I got older. I feel guilty that I survived. Grandfather, Grandmother, and Mother were all in deep sorrow and dismay, but their mourning somehow reproached me. Why didn't I die? Why did he die, and not I? Their tears accused me as though Hamnet's death were my fault...
Will	No, Judith, no.
Judith	You didn't come to the funeral. Mother waited for

you.

Will

Judith   And you only love Susanna. She is smart. I…

Will

Judith   I am still a maid, not married.

Will   Judith, you do not have to marry. You may live with us as we are now. I speak sincerely. We may live together as long as you wish.

Judith is surprised at Will's words.

Judith   What did you say? We, live together? I don't have to marry?

Will   Just so. As now — your mother, and you and I.

Judith   My God! If you speak truly, then I, I will go to London.

Will   *(surprised)* To London?

Judith   Yes, I want to live alone there as you did. There is no man who wants me here in Stratford, and there is no man I want. I will not marry.

Will   There is merit in living unmarried. I do not object. Marriage is no one's duty. But…

Judith   *(Interrupting)* … You will let me go then?

Will looks at Judith, holds her hand and embraces her warmly. She
returns the embrace without a word.

Will   Judith... Hamnet.

VO is heard in the dim sound of the bell.

VO   "To die to sleep;
          No more; and by a sleep, to say we end
          The heart-ache and thousand natural shocks
          That flesh is heir to, 'tis a consummation
          Devoutly to be wished. To die, to sleep —"

          The Earth and the universe
          You and I too,
          All things vanish into air, into the aether,
          Without a trace.
          "We are such stuff
          As dreams are made on and our little life
          Is rounded with sleep."

The church bell is still heard.

[Act 2]

⟨Scene 1⟩

New Place and The Avon

1614

Will is sitting on an old wooden bench at the river. He is looking at the swans. The white swans and blue river make a beautiful landscape; the river now reflects a pinkish sunset. Will looks tired. Inside New Place, Susanna and Judith speak.

Will   Quiet here. The banks of the Thames' were raving mad. Roaring bears, barking dogs, and baying humans. The place was rife with savage noise. I prefer this quiet of the Avon.

Susanna   Judith, you don't know, do you? The neighboring women asked me, "Where did your father go?" "When will he return?" "What does he do in London?" They always teased me as a child. Sometimes they stared at me sneering. I remember. They never dared it with Mother, though.

Judith	I know it. Why do you think only you know? Presumptuous girl!
Susanna	*(laughing)* You were teased too?
Judith	Yes. I spat and threw a small stone once at the end of my patience. Then they called me wicked.
Susanna	*(laughing)* I didn't know that. Ha ha, yes you were a wicked girl. But I didn't know that was the reason they called you that.
Judith	You didn't protect me, did you? Sometimes you teased me along with them.
Susanna	You didn't need my protection. You were a strong, nasty child, weren't you? You never treated me as your elder. You rarely addressed me as "Sister," or even "Susanna." I was merely "You" or "She," as though I were the younger. You still do it now.
Judith	*(jokingly)* You, you, you, Susanna.
Susanna	*(jokingly)* Judith, wretched girl, grow up.
Will	What am I doing here? The old king who chose the time to retire, he with his three daughters. He kept reminding me of the day I myself would meet soon enough. Inevitably I surrendered to him, and so I returned to the place of my birth. My pleasure now is sitting here at the river and viewing the swans. I

practice at becoming an old country squire, who has forgotten how to write. Like old Lear, three women are with me, though one is a wife.

Judith   Learned sister Susanna, have you read any of it, by any chance?

Susanna   One or two. So many difficult words. I didn't understand them all. I doubt the Londoners can understand his words either.

Judith   Tell me about a play you read.

Susanna   Read? Well, no, how can I read it myself? But I listened to John's reading. Very beautiful. I've never heard such wonderful and elegant language in my life. It was Romeo and Juliet. The lovers! They fall in love at first sight. Imagine that!

Judith   Do they? Father told me once that we are in his plays.

Susanna   He told me too. I wonder whose love story it is then?

Judith   How does the love story go? Do they marry?

Susanna   Yes, they marry, but secretly.

Judith   A secret marriage?

Susanna   Their two houses had been enemies for a long time.

Judith   They marry? Though their families are enemies? It must have a sad ending, then?

Susanna	The lovers kill themselves. Sad but beautiful.
Will	I thought I had forgotten all... But the places I encounter here stir the memories... memories of our primal scenes. I never expected that. The place I first met Anne. I pass it in my walk. The place of our first kiss. Was it at the river? Was it the Forest of Arden? Ah, it was a summer night. Why did I go into the woods? Was I following her? I don't remember. I only remember her white shoulder reflecting the moonlight. I kissed it.
Susanna	They are very young. Juliet is fourteen, Romeo sixteen. They are mere children. I have wondered whether these young lovers are my parents. Was their love story baked into the play? They fall in love as soon as they meet. I think Romeo is a fairly ordinary young boy, while Juliet is mature and positive. So was Mother when she met Father, wasn't she?
Judith	Was she?
Susanna	Romeo is more attracted by Juliet's beauty. I see him as a common boy, like many. But Juliet drinks a potion that may kill her. How courageous! How does she do it! She is only fourteen.

Judith	She drinks poison?
Susanna	Imagine Mother. She could marry the man she wanted. Her parents were dead already, so nobody could interfere with her marriage. She was pretty, she had some inherited money, so she herself could choose, in spite of his being younger than she.
Judith	She must have been the best bride to be found in Shottery and Stratford, though she was quite old to marry.
Susanna	*(laughing)* As you are?
Judith	*(laughing)* As I am, yes. And as you were, I believe.
Susanna	Yes, but with a rich and famous father, so I met John. Mother was younger than you when she married. *(giggles)* Father might have been mature for his age. The girls his age were too young for him. It is certain that they spoke different languages.
Will	It was Puck's jest. He played a joke on us that night. He put a drop of love potion into my eyes. The fire of passion possessed me. So vivid and true. The woman was beautiful and I was in her arms.
Judith	He would have been attracted by mother's fair looks, like Romeo.
Susanna	Can you guess what Juliet's first thoughts were upon

	meeting Romeo?
Judith	What? To marry?
Susanna	Right! To marry. Mother must have felt that same urgency to marry.
Judith	*(staring)* Are you mocking me now?
Susanna	*(Sarcastically)* Heavens, no! Why would I? *(Now more sincerely)* You will not marry, will you?
Will	Shooting stars fell often that summer. Perhaps I went to Arden Forest to see them.
Susanna	Do you want to hear? I memorized some lines because they were so moving.

(She recites)

"If that thy bent of love be honorable,

Thy purpose marriage, send me word tomorrow,

By one that I'll procure to come to thee,

Where and what time thou wilt perform the rite,

And all my fortunes at thy foot I'll lay,

And follow thee my lord throughout the world."

See? It is Juliet who first proposes to marry instantly, tomorrow.

| Judith | "I will follow thee my lord throughout the world." |

They break into laughter looking at one another.

Mother did it. She has lived only waiting for Father.

Susanna Yes, she has. But the love between them didn't last, it seems. They were separated too long.

Judith Twenty-eight years.

Susanna Judith, do you know that I have always had a suspicion he must have had a lover in London?

Judith You're right. It would be a lie that he could live without a lover for so long.

Susanna The theatre world is open only for men, all male actors, all male writers, and all male patrons. Well, the whole world is for men only.

Judith I've never heard of women actors, women writers. Have you?

Susanna Do not be surprised... yes I have. I know of one.

Judith *(surprised and unbelieving)* What? Truthfully?

Susanna Emilia.

Judith Emilia? Who is she?

Susanna Emilia Lanier[2]. She published a book in London. I

---

2) Emilia Lanier(1569-1654) is the first female professional poet in England. Her book *Salve Deus Rex Judaerum* was printed in 1613. The

heard she is a poet. Extraordinary, isn't it? A woman
wrote a book!

Judith   Yes, it's extraordinary, but difficult to believe! She
even published! She must know how to read and
write like the best of men, then. Was she Father's
lover? Is that what you mean?

Susanna She must be intelligent and worldly. She would be
a well-known lady in London. Father must have
known her. She came to see plays in Father's theatre,
I suppose.

Judith suddenly starts to cry.

Susanna What is this about? Judith?

Judith   He left us illiterate.

Susanna That's why you cry? She is a most excellent woman.
Different from us! She is an exception. There's no
way for girls like us. Don't you know that? I knew
it when I was young. So I obeyed, marrying without
complaint.

---

poem "Eve's Apology in Defence of Women" is in it. She is thought
to be a "Dark Lady" and now considered to be a proto-Feminist
poet. She also is one of the candidates of "Shakespeare Authorship
Controversy."

Judith   What are we? Our father is the best writer for the stage, a poet, an actor, the famous William Shakespeare! We, however, can't read and write, rustic country girls! I write my name only in sign. It is cruel. Girls can't go to school either.

Susanna   How I was envious as Uncle Edmund[3] went to school with Hamnet every morning! Yes, it's most clear; he could go to school because he was a boy. The difference between man and woman. Judith, you must learn letters and learn to write. Never mind such a thing as marriage. Mother never imagined he would be a famous writer. Nor did we. Nobody in Stratford did. So we shouldn't be any more astonished if you published a book in ten years like Emilia.

The noisy crying of birds is heard. Will gets up and looks down the bank. A herd of swans in panic run to the water fluttering. A sick, shaking swan is seen left behind. Thomas Quiney appears and hesitates to say hello to Will. He now comes closer, realizing something is happening.

Thomas   Ah, Sir, what is the matter?

---

3) Shakespeare's youngest brother.

The swan is breathing hard and suffering. Thomas observes it.

Oh, hell!

Will   It seems the wings are broken.

Thomas   Old swan, anyway. Yes, it must be wounded. The wings are broken.

The two men don't know what to do, but just watch. At last the swan dies with a last cry.

Thomas   Dead. Damn.

Will   *(Looks at Thomas, surprised by his vulgarity.)*

Thomas   Ah, Master Shakespeare. So good to see you. I am Thomas.

Will   *(unable to remember)* Thomas?

Thomas   Yes, Thomas Quiney. The vint…

Will   … Oh, Quiney, yes… The wine merchant. Is it truly dead?

Thomas   It is a very old swan. Too old to live. Never mind.

Will   *(lost in thought)*

Thomas   Sir?

Will   Dead, then.

Thomas	Sir?
Will	Hm... Yes, Richard Quiney, your father. I met him once in London.
Thomas	You did. You reminded me of him. He passed on ten years ago.
Will	Already?

(silence)

Thomas	I lived in London briefly. I inherited the business from my father. I ran a wine establishment. I have a wine tavern in High Street. I am on my way there.
Will	A tavern? I see. How old are you?
Thomas	I am twenty-five. How are you getting along, Sir? You're doing alright in the country? How is Anne?
Will	We are well.
Thomas	Please come to my tavern some time. I'll treat you to our best wine.
Will	
Thomas	*(uncomfortable at getting no reaction)* It's getting dark. The sun has set. I must go now. It is an honor to meet you here and see you again. God be with you.

Thomas bows and leaves. On his way he turns around and looks at

Will.

Thomas *(aside)* He is a rich man now. And a gentleman too! Did I behave well? I called his wife Anne. Was that foolish? Should I have said "Madam" or "your lady"? It sounds awkward. Damn it, I know her very well; we are neighbors. Mother and she have known each other for a long time. It's not easy to call her Madam all of a sudden. I know he is famous in London. All we Stratfordians know that. He said that he met my father in London. That's news to me. Did Father borrow money from him? He had a debt of £30 some years ago. Did Shakespeare meet him to lend him money?... I don't know. It is an old story. I don't want to delve into it further...

Will *(He turns to observe Thomas, who is walking away)* Twenty-five? Then he is younger than Hamnet. Four or five years younger. Why am I judging his age compared to Hamnet's?

Just before Thomas leaves, he takes a glance at Judith. Judith feels his eyes and turns back to see him. Their eyes meet. Thomas, embarrassed, hurriedly exits.

⟨Scene 2⟩

Stratford

Hall's Croft

1614–1615

John   Your father has a lot of land in and around Stratford. If the land is enclosed for sheep the income will double.

Susanna   London and its theatres must be a wonder. I am astounded by how much money one may earn there.

John   London is the largest city in Europe, you know. Its population is enormous. It has the most theatres in Europe. Perhaps ten or so at the Thames. Many writers and actors are needed to populate the stages. There are more than ten theatre companies, I suppose. They will soon rebuild the Globe. Your father will be asked to write again. The audience wants to see new works.

Susanna   Father has retired. He will not go to London again.

John   He seems to live his old age ideally. He is a healthy and rich old man! Besides, he lives near a loving daughter, whom he can see whenever he likes.

That's the most favorable thing for him. I think that is the reason he returned, is it not?

Susanna   Yes, Father's love for me is special.

John   You are Cordelia, aren't you? *(laughing)* By the way, are they still cold toward each other? I don't know what to say...

Susanna   Father tries...

John Hall

Susanna   You know that Grandfather lost his post as a bailiff, and got into debt, many years ago.

John   Yes I know.

Susanna   His business went down suddenly.

John   The luxurious glove business fell on hard times as the general prosperity deteriorated. He was unfortunate.

Susanna   Father wanted to recover his fortunes as a son. John Shakespeare was unlucky and failed, but his son Will succeeded in London and became a rich man. He wanted to hear that. Nothing else.

John   He has his coat of arms, and has become a gentleman. He is one of the richest men in Stratford. A proud and respectable man. I too am proud of him. How fortunate you are! The elder daughter he loves most.

(He kisses her on her cheek.)

You will inherit all of his assets. Lands, houses, and even the new house in London.

Susanna   Do not forget Judith.

John   *(laughing)* I know, I don't mean anything. I am self-sufficient. It does not matter to me. It's not my concern where his wealth goes. You know that I am doing well as a physician. People trust me. It is enough for me.

Susanna   Yes, yes, I know that. You are a prestigious doctor.

John   *(gestures like a knight)* Madam, my gratitude!

Susanna   *(gestures as a noble lady)* Sir, you are most welcome!

John   Humbly, may I ask a question, Madam?

Susanna   *(smiles)* I permit it.

John   Why did your father purchase a house in London just before he returned home? He had stayed in London a long time without a house, though he could have owned one. He remained as a lodger. I am curious about this. Aren't you?

Susanna   I talked about it with Judith. We were curious too. Returning home was most certain, and then he bought a house. Why? Incredibly, Judith has her eye on it; she wants to go to London and live in that house.

John	Is that so? Not to marry?
Susanna	She will not. She will live unmarried. So she wants to go to London. She intends to pursue a life there, as Father did.
John	*(cynical laughing)* A respectable young woman by herself in London? Im... possible.
Susanna	Father and Mother won't permit it. It's only Judith's hope... impossible.
	(silence)
	Well, anyway, the farmers will lose their land if it is enclosed, and then where will they go? The poor farmers, without land for crops?
John	They will go to the city and become cheap labourers. That's why the number of poor city-dwellers is increasing. I don't know what your father thinks about it, but the enclosure movement cannot be stopped now. Father can't resist it.
Susanna	The farmers' protest movement grows strong. I am worried.
John	Do not worry. Many people are involved; the landowners. William Comb and William Replingham[4]

---

4) They were the central people of the movement. Shakespeare kept his tithes by making a contract with them.

will not give up their income from the land. They will try to keep the tithes, although they would enclose their land.

Susanna

John   I don't see him often nowadays.

Susanna How does he look to you?

John   It seems he likes taking a walk at the river... he just looks like an ordinary old man in the country, as though he had lived here all along. I think he is adjusting himself well, don't you?

Susanna

John   Stratford may be foreign to him because he lived in London for more than twenty years. He might have to learn to be familiar.

Susanna He doesn't look special or different but... I don't believe it sometimes. He was an outstanding figure in the London theatrical world. Most of his plays succeeded and were performed at court. He was the finest playwright and a favorite of Queen Elizabeth and King James!

John   How can he help getting old? He invented new words and unique expressions. He perfected the style of so-called blank verse in his plays. Such great

	literary achievements! But now he must quietly sit back, waiting for the end... as all men do.
Susanna	He is over fifty. He becomes weak, inevitably. By the way, John, how is it that you know so much about his plays? Blank verse? What is that?
John	(smile) I am his great admirer. It's difficult to see his plays on stage but I try to get the quartos whenever they are published. If a patient goes to London, I ask him to buy them for me. I have read most of his tragedies. As a matter of fact, I plan to write a medical book myself. I find it very challenging. Inventing sentences? Phew, so much work. Your father has a genius!
Susanna	(smile) Wonderful! I am glad to hear your plan to write a book.
John	(laughing) Don't expect too much. It will happen in the distant future.
Susanna	Would you please read another play for me?
John	If you wish. Alright, this time, how about *King Lear*?
Susanna	I like it, whatever it is.
John	Then we shall read *King Lear*.
Susanna	For me it is not easy to match the great writer with the old man sitting at the river. Do you know what I

mean?

John   Hm…

Susanna   Are they the same person? The busiest writer and actor in London theatres, and the old man at the river looking at swans?

John   You mean…

Susanna   The land he purchased. Uncle Gilbert did it on Father's behalf while he was in London.

John   Susanna dear, tell me what you are thinking.

Susanna   He purchased another farm lately. I am afraid it may appear to you that he has an excessive desire for land, and to accumulate wealth.

(silence)

It seems to me that it's an effort to compensate a feeling of emptiness. Does he really need another farm? For what? He already has enough land.

John   Yes.

Susanna   His passion for the stage, his essence as a writer, his reality, all have disappeared. I think the purchasing behaviour arises out of that hole in his spirit. It is his effort to be a real country gentleman, his desire to bridge the gap between himself and his wife and daughters. It is another way of defining himself.

He knew what he was doing and I think he already knew it was meaningless as well.

John   *(touched by her sensitivity)* I've never thought of it that way. You are a good daughter. He is a well-blessed father.

Susanna   Now I understand why he left us, why he stayed in London so long. It is impossible to ignore newly discovered talents.

⟨Scene 3⟩

Arden Forest

Summer

1615

Anne and Judith pick flowers in the woods.

VO   *(song)*

"I know a bank where the wild thyme blows,

Where oxlips and nodding violet grows,

Quite over-canopied with luscious woodbine,

With sweet musk-roses and with eglantine;

There sleeps Titania sometime of the night.

Lull'd in these flowers with dances and delight..."

Judith   Mother, here are violets and wild thyme. Oh, woodbine — so many purples, each with different petals.

Anne   Pretty, and here are sweet musk roses.

Judith   That's your favorite. We have them in our garden too.

Two women with hats and baskets are busy picking flowers. Bees and butterflies are sucking nectar; birds are singing. Anne spreads a blanket on the grass and prepares lunch for them. A bunch of flowers is set aside.

Anne   We should bring Elizabeth. I haven't seen her for a while. She must have grown since last I saw her.

Judith   She resembles her clever mother. Elizabeth has learnt the alphabet already.

Anne   Oh? How brilliant she is! Her parents are eager to teach her, aren't they?

Judith   John teaches her to read, of course.

Anne   Your father can teach you. Would you like to learn?

Judith	No I would not. He is not home; he always wanders about near the river bank.
Anne	Judith, are you uncomfortable with Father?
Judith	That's what I would like to ask you, Mother. Are you comfortable? I don't think so.
Anne	He is... not the man I used to know.
Judith	He was young then. I don't know him either. I've seen him only a couple of times, when I was little. He was quiet and didn't say a word. As I remember, I had the feeling he was afraid of you then.
Anne	Was he afraid of me? Why?
Judith	Because he abandoned us... he left you.
Anne	
Judith	Why do you think he left?

Anne is embarrassed by this unexpected question and her hand begins to shake. She tries to hide it with the other hand.

Judith	*(seeing the shaking hand)* Mother...
	(silence)
Judith	I am sorry, Mother.
Anne	No, no, it's alright. He became a father all of a sudden, so he was very much confused. A man does

not experience a birth in his own body. I thought he couldn't quite believe he had become a father.

Judith   *(still conscious of Anne's hand)* If he had refused to marry you and had run away, what would have happened to you?

Anne   He might have. Had he done so, he wouldn't have been able to return to Stratford.

Judith   And what about you, Mother?

Anne   Me? I would be an unwed mother, and Susanna a bastard. All contempt and despite I should have to endure. I might have hidden myself just at the outskirts of a village. I would be lucky not to be condemned as a witch.

Judith   You could have raised Susanna by yourself. You had some money inherited from Grandfather. But you could not avoid scandals and scorn. Or you could have left for some other village or a city where nobody knew you. You could have been hired as a maid by a wealthy family, or become a cheap labourer, or a washerwoman. But then who could take care of the child?

Anne   The infant would likely have gone to an orphanage.

(smiles)

Judith	Mother, did you ever think of aborting the child? You would just get rid of the pregnancy and leave for London.
Anne	*(looking straight in Judith's eyes)* I never thought of that. Not only the baby but also I myself could have been killed. It is a very very dangerous thing. This was my first child. It might have been the first and last opportunity to be a mother. To marry or not would not have mattered.
Judith	*(surprised)*
Anne	The process of the marriage has been long and difficult. In truth, your father has run away. Not right after the wedding but three years on. He caught the perfect time.
Judith	*(sighing)* Mother, how did you endure living alone with three young children?
Anne	Judith, why do we speak of this now, on such a beautiful day?

She looks up at the sky. A tear falls down her cheek. The sky is reflected in the tear. Her hand shakes again.

Judith	I watched Father return to London – watched you live

in loneliness again in a new house. I saw everything.
I saw him return home again – and saw that he was
also lonely and solitary. I see it everyday.

Anne

Judith   Mother, he won't leave again, he will grow old with
you.

Anne

Judith   Father's house in London... Mother.

Anne

Judith   May I go to live there? I want to live freely, I won't
marry. I'll go to theatres and see the performances.
Why must a woman live like this? The only thing
to do is marry. Nothing else. Women have souls and
freedom. Women are God's creatures too, aren't
they?

Anne   Women are not supposed to think that way, as you
know. That's why we are prohibited from education
in the schools.

*Margaret and Mary appear on the other side of the woods. Anne and
Judith hear the footsteps but pay no attention to them. The village
girls do not notice Anne and Judith. Margaret is in her mid-twenties,
Mary in her early twenties. They are smelling the flowers and*

humming songs. Then the girls begin to sing. The songs are from Hamlet.

Margaret *(song)*

     "Tomorrow is Saint Valentine's day,

     All in the morning betime,

     And I a maid at your window,

     To be your Valentine.

     Then up he rose, and donn'd his clo'es,

     And dupped the chamber-door,

     Let in the maid, that out a maid

     Never departed more."

Mary *(song)*

     "By Gis and by Saint Charity,

     Alack and fie for shame,

     Young men will do't if they come to't -

     By Cock, they are to blame,

     Quoth she, 'Before you tumbled me,

     You promise me to wed."

The two girls, laughing and singing, exit on the other side of the woods. The sound of their laughter remains on the stage.

[Act 3]

⟨Scene 1⟩

The Avon

Early Winter

1615

Will is sitting on a bench. He looks cold and lonely. He has gotten old. The sun is setting. The sky and the river gradually turn red-orange. Will is looking down at the swans.

Will   The swans' movements are elegant and dignified. I wish no more than to end my life that way.

(pause)

The men in my tragedies die miserably... such is tragedy of course. *(bitter smile)* Romeo was the death of youth; Hamlet, Laertes, the death of young manhood; Macbeth, Caesar, Othello, the death of middle age; Lear, the old man's death. I prefer that a man should discover his foolishness before his death, regardless of his years. Lear is over eighty.

(pause)

I must see my foolishness... I long to warm her mind... and to lay down the burden in my own... before my ending.

Judith enters. She puts a soft blanket on Will's shoulder.

Will	*(feels the blanket and smiles)* You are Cordelia.
Judith	*(smile)* You are King Lear?
Will	Yes, well, no. I am not a foolish old man.
Judith	*(sits beside him)* It's cold.
Will	It is. The swans are shivering too. The small birds have flown away to find their nests.
Judith	Is it true that all the swans belong to the Queen?
Will	Ben used to call me "The swan of the Avon." A number of swans in this river.
Judith	Father, you know what? The swans live with only one partner and raise their babies together.
Will	
Judith	
Will	The old man believed Cordelia would stay with him. He was wrong.
Judith	Your Cordelia was Susanna. She has gone. Have I

replaced her?

Will *(smile)* You won't leave.

Judith You're afraid of being alone with mother, aren't you?

Will

Judith

Will Your mother is an icy wall.

Judith Her true mind will prove different. You must wait a little longer.

Will No time remains.

 (silence)

Judith I'll be with you, Father.

Will *(relieved)* Not in London.

Judith I'll live there for just three years.

Will But you just said you would stay with me.

Judith

Will

Judith Father, I have a favour to ask.

Will I said no to London.

Judith No, my… letters. Teach me how to write.

Will *(a small laugh)*

Judith Will you?

Will For what purpose?

Judith	I want to read *King Lear* with my own knowledge. I want to read all of your plays. I also wish to write a book, like the woman poet.
Will	*(surprised)* The woman poet?
Judith	She published a book. Her name is Emilia Lanier. You know her, don't you?
Will	Oh, I've heard of a book or two by a woman. They might be forgotten amid the noise and gossip.
Judith	*(surprised and a bit angry)* Forgotten amid the gossip? Such a book was absolutely published!
Will	So many books are published. Obscurity is the destiny of common books. They are cast into the sea of words.
Judith	The world is not fair. This is not a common book. It should be remembered... I want to read it too. *(pauses)* She must have visited your theatre often, I am sure.
Will.	
Judith	There are women who dress as men in your plays. Their model might have been Emilia the poet. Did you create those characters thinking of her?
Will	*(surprised and tries to hide his embarrassment)*
Judith	Did they dress as men in order to say what they had

to say, because they could never have said it or been heard otherwise?

Will Who told you such a thing?

Judith Dr. John Hall, a learned man.

Will Did he?

Judith Women can't say a word to the world. Will this change in a century?

Will You have heard of my Portia, then?

Judith Yes, Portia defeats the Jew in the Venetian court. She is remarkable, excellent, talented! But she is not she. She must be concealed by a man's dress. For women, wit and talent and intelligence only become curses! When will this world change, so that Portia does not need to wear a man's clothes?

Will

Judith It is no different for the noble women. They have wealth and status, but no poets, no actors, nothing. Alas, this woman poet should be remembered and acclaimed widely.

Will Judith…

Judith Might it be different if a woman were queen? But no, even Queen Elizabeth did not alter these circumstances.

Will *(smiles and hugs her shoulder with one arm)* Then

you must live differently. My daughter, you do not have to marry. Live in that world of a hundred years hence. But on one condition; that you stay with me forever.

Judith   Father.

Will   *(releases the hug and examines her face)*

Will   You are Cordelia, aren't you.

Judith   Cordelia too goes to France with her husband. But I won't go with a husband. I don't need a man. If I go, I'll go alone, not following anyone.

Will   *(uncomfortable)*

Judith   Let me go to London.

Will   No!

Judith   I will go.

Will   *(stands up and yells.)* No!

Father and daughter stare at each other as the tension rises. After a while, Judith furiously gets up and swiftly runs off. Will stands still in silence.

The thin, bare branches look cold and lonely.

⟨Scene 2⟩

Will's Room

New Place

January 1616

Will is writing his will. He looks much older and weaker. We can see the contents of the will on the screen at the rear of the stage. It is a part of the existing will.

Francis Collins[5], a solicitor and overseer, is sitting on a chair at a slight distance in the room, and Will is lost in thought.

Will   Now I can count my remaining days. The last could be today or tomorrow. I must finish this while I still have strength.

          (stops writing)

          The Gatehouse in London. Yes, that house is in a good area, Blackfriars. Judith wanted to stay there… but I wouldn't allow it. How could I permit her to go alone to a great metropolis like London? It is too

---

5) Fransis Collins is Will's friend and helped him to purchase lands. As a overseer, he dictated and executed the will. The other overseer is Thomas Russell.

dangerous and too crowded... a father's mind.

(pause)

I have almost forgotten why I bought it. I suppose I thought I might visit often, meeting with my dear theatre friends and watching them on the stage. And the new plays, whoever is writing them... And... the noble man. Only to see him I wished to go to London. But I could not go. I never imagined I would stay in Stratford like a native.

(pause)

The lodging houses in Southwark occupy my thoughts. The area was not wealthy or clean, the neighbors migrants and small shop owners. The brothels were within a few steps. I lodged in a couple of houses, and could not remove myself from the area. In truth, I enjoyed living among foreigners. Edward lived nearby, but I was too busy to attend to him. I regretted his death sorely. I held a pretty decent funeral as penance for my carelessness as an elder brother. He is buried in Southwark Cathedral. An actor but an unlucky man.

(pause)

The landlord in Silver Street was a Huguenot.

He might have been one of the refugees from the Massacre in France, though he would not say, and I had no heart to ask.[6] My room upstairs had a desk, a chair, and a bed, that was all. No books. I wrote at night. The candle dripped its tears on my desk, and I wrote and wrote on my paper. My fingers were dyed in ink, the middle one thick with callus.

(holds up his hand and looks at his fingers)

If I had bought my own house there for writing, I could have worked in more comfortable surroundings. *(bitter smile)* Instead, I bought this house, New Place.

(pause)

My life in London was busy and passionate. I was alive when I imagined scenes and threw them instantly to the actors, who would recite them grandly on the stage. Burbage was excellent. He was transformed into the characters immediately. I revelled in my invention! We were all alive in the Globe.

(silence)

But in truth, I was already dead as I was writing

---

6) Massacre of Saint Bartholomew Day, in France.

Henry VIII. An empty codpiece, as Lear's fool says. My imagination had dried out then. I was a pathetic shadow, a walking shadow, as Macbeth laments. I knew it well.

(Writes)

I bequeath this house to Susanna. Judith? She won't marry and won't go to London. No, I won't let it happen. She will be here after I die and will live with Anne. Susanna would not expel them from the house. I will bequeath to Judith £300... the house in Chapel St... and the large silver-gilt bowl.

(writes)

All my assets, all the real estate to Susanna. She has no son; the family line may not be continued.

(pause)

A little plot for a coffin and a piece of cloth to wrap a body... that's enough, in truth. Why did I aspire to possess more and more?

(pause)

My plays? I leave them as a gift to those who love the theatre. I do not know how long they will be performed. They might soon be forgotten along with my death... or survive beyond time.

(silence)

Will is old. He is exhausted from writing. He finishes and puts down his quill. Collins comes closer, reads through the papers, and gestures to Will to sign. Will looks up at Collins' eyes, puts his quill into the ink pot, and writes his name on each page. The lawyer checks and confirms. He nods.

⟨Scene 3⟩

New Place

February 1616

There is a tense atmosphere among the three women.

Susanna　The wedding ceremony cannot be done, Judith, you know that. Lent will soon begin, so you will have to wait until Easter.

Judith　After the third of April? No, I cannot wait two months.

Anne　*(sees and touches Judith's belly, nervously)* Judith, are you...?

Judith	No, Mother, don't think of it. I am not.
Anne	Then why are you in such a hurry to marry?
Susanna	Only two months, Judith. Then you may marry with everyone's blessing.
Judith	No... he is urging me... it can't wait.
Susanna	*(laughing)* If that is so, then you must get a special licence from the Bishop of Worcester. Besides, you have to participate in a church meeting twice. Can you do these things? It's not easy. Do you really want to proceed with such a wedding?
Judith	
Anne	Judith, you seem to be repeating my marriage. If you are not with child, why are you so stubborn? I had to get a licence from the bishop. You know that.
Judith	Mother, I am sorry... I don't know why, but I just want to do... just want to do it... soon...
Susanna	*(burst of laughter)* Are you playing a game of "Romeo and Juliet"? At your age, you have fallen in love? Judith, have you forgotten London? You said you wouldn't marry; you would go to London.
Judith	Susanna, please, go upstairs and talk to Father, would you?
Susanna	*(kidding)* Call me "Sister."

Judith   *(hesitates)* Of course... my dear sister Susanna.

Susanna stares at Judith half-mockingly. Anne gives her a nod. Susanna goes to Will's room. He is sitting in an armchair, looking older and weaker than ever.

Susanna   Father, how are you?

Will

Susanna   I'll bring John to you.

Will   No, I am alright.

Susanna takes a careful look at Will. He doesn't look alright.

Susanna   *(trying to cheer him)* Father, I have good news.

Will

Susanna   Judith... Judith will marry.

Will   *(surprised and unbelieving)* What? Marry? What do you mean?

Susanna   Yes, she will.

Will   Judith? Why? So sudden... with whom?

Susnna   Father, she is thirty-one. There is no eligible man older than she in Stratford. It is still harder to find one younger.

Will	So…
Susanna	The younger man is… Thomas. Thomas Quiney.
Will	Richard Quiney's son?
Susanna	Yes. He has been in London, and learnt how to do business.
Will	
Susanna	In High Street, he…
Will	… I know.
Susanna	Judith was once the most desirable bride in and around Stratford. Her father was a famous writer and rich man. Many men may have wanted her, thinking of her inheritance. But she is not young anymore…
Will	No, no, no….
Susanna	Father, we have known Thomas since he was little. He is not like those men who only seek money. Judith is not frivolous either.
Will	I don't believe it. No, Susanna, go and tell her to come.
Susanna	Father, she is afraid to face you, but she is determined.

Susanna leaves and Judith enters in a moment. Will tries to sit up straight.

Will	
Judith	
Will	Judith.
Judith	Father.
Will	Is it true?
Judith	Yes.
Will	Do you love him?
Judith	*(hesitating)* Perhaps.
Will	
Judith	
Will	You will leave me.

(silence)

Will	We agreed that you didn't have to marry, did we not? We would live here, your mother and you and I, all three together.
Judith	I have nothing to say, Father.
Will	Are you Cordelia, then? No, no – you won't speak?
Judith	I cannot heave my heart into my mouth.
Will	You said you would stay with me.
Judith	
Will	
Judith	You didn't allow me to go to London, so I will marry as I wish. There is nothing else left that I may do

according to my desire. Who knows? Thomas may allow me to go to London after marriage. Or he and I may go together. He will be different from you.

Will   Judith, you, earnestly…

Judith   *(stops him)* Father, he is not eighteen, he is twenty-seven.

Will   *(bitter smile)*

Judith   You thought of me as Cordelia. She, the loving daughter, could not stay with her father forever.

Will   She was banished. You are not. I will never banish you. You won't marry, Judith, no, Cordelia.

Judith   We will marry even though it is Lent. You will not permit me but I do not need your permission. It is my marriage.

Will   *(furious, he stands up)* You, you, you are not Cordelia. You are Desdemona who deceives her father.

Judith   Desdemona says this, doesn't she, when she chooses Othello?

"Here's my husband;
And so much duty I may profess
Due to the Moor my lord."

Will   No, don't, you… you are not my daughter!

Will falls down in the chair. Silence. Judith looks down at Will for a
long time.

Judith   "We are not the first who with best meaning have
            incurred the worst."
            I will go to London.

Anne enters and Judith exits. Now Anne watches Will for a while.

Anne   Will.

Will raises his head and sees Anne. He is surprised and doesn't
understand why she is here.

Anne   Did you forget? Judith is me thirty years ago. I only
          hope that Thomas will not leave her alone.
Will   I left because…
Anne   You left, yes… I don't care now, whatever the
          reason.
Will   I returned.
Anne   You returned because your remaining days were

short. When you had a great many days to live, you ran away. Now you must watch Judith as she lives her many days.

Anne's arm and hand begin to shake. As Will notices it, Anne exits. Will painfully opens his mouth and speaks but it is barely audible.

Will   She is… her hand… her hand… *(mourns)*
(pause)
Is there a happily married couple in my plays?… No, none. *Macbeth*? Only their ambition and desire unite them. Living together a long time as man and wife is another story. The true couple conforms to one another, mind and body; they share a spiritual intimacy. We call this "the happy marriage."
If Romeo and Juliet had not died, if they had lived long? Unimaginable. They love for only eight days and then die.
The couples I conceived were all isolated and disconnected. Goneril and Albany. Goneril is lonely and wants love; Albany doesn't know and can't give it. He is a fool, a piece of wood. Desdemona and Othello… Hermione and Leontes… A happy

couple? None. O Anne... O Judith, my Cordelia...

⟨Scene 4⟩

Half Moon in the night sky

15 March, 1616

Yellow half Moon. A thrush chirps feebly.

Anne   A bird singing at night. You are alone. You have lost

someone.

(listening to the birdsong.)

Why do you cry? Do you miss your lover?

I wish I could cry as you do.

Those years of loneliness...

He returned

But he is not the man I loved

My cheeks were reddish yesterday

Today my hair has turned white

(approaches the bird)

Come

Come here

I'll hold you.

She holds the bird on her hand gently. Her hand is shaking a bit. The bird seems wounded, can't fly, and walks limpingly. Anne hugs it warmly to her bosom. The bird looks up at her eyes, its body trembling.

Anne   Yes, yes.

Are you hurt?

Are you hungry?

Do you miss your lover?

Don't weep…

(strokes the bird)

You little thing, you are shaking

Poor little thing

Do you know?

(strokes the bird)

My daughter is in the same circumstance as I

thirty years ago.

The poor girl is like me thirty years ago.

A painful cry of childbirth overlaps the bird's weak song. Anne is frozen by the woman's scream. Margaret is in labour. Her mother

Joan and a midwife are seen. With them Mary is crying. This scene is proceeding behind a translucent curtain. We see only their silhouettes.

Anne is down stage, before the curtain, listening to all the cries and talk.

Joan   Margaret, Margaret, what can I do? *(to the midwife)* Come and help, help her!

Midwife   Not yet. Margaret, tell me, tell me the name. Who is the baby's father? Then I can help you!

Margaret is in great pain. She is swallowing her cries and shouting loudly.

Joan   *(to the midwife)* You're killing my daughter. Help her, please, help. A name? What's that! Not important! Save her and the child... please!

Midwife   Come Margaret, you and your baby will be safe if you name him. Say the father's name. I can't help you unless you say it. I was ordered. Poor thing! Mary, you know it, you tell me.

Mary   No, I don't know it! *(weeping)*

Margaret loses herself and comes back for a while as the pain reaches climax.

Joan   I can't bear anymore. I'll help her, I can't kill my daughter. You get away! You're so cruel.

Joan tries to help her daughter's childbirth, but the midwife stops her. The two women struggle.

Anne   Why, why... why don't you speak out? You are not to blame for it. You are innocent. The whole village knows and hushes it up. Only we didn't know it, Margaret. I know the name. It is Thomas. The baby's father is Thomas, Thomas Quiney. My Judith's husband. Thomas should marry poor Margaret. We won't make you an unmarried mother and your baby a bastard. Margaret, say it! Say the name... Thomas Quiney!

(Women's cries and weeping, Margaret's howling.)

The midwife is so cruel and mad that she does not move a finger! Who ordered her not to help until the girl confessed the name? Please help her deliver the child safely. I'll adopt the baby if possible. Oh, poor thing. God in your benevolence, make all safe and unharmed!

Margaret *(shouts)* Thomas… Thomas… Quiney…

The sounds disappear, leaving all suddenly in silence. At once, Margaret's scream tears the silence. A baby is born, but its first cry is not heard. Now Joan's cry is heard, implying Margaret's death. Anne falls down.

Music fades in and envelops the women's cries. Ophelia's song, sung by Margaret's voice, is heard through the music.

VO "Tomorrow is Saint Valentine's day,

All in the morning betime,

And I a maid at your window,

To be your Valentine.

Then up he rose, and donn'd his clo'es,

And dupped the chamber-door,

Let in the maid, that out a maid

Never departed more."

Anne lowers her head and cries. The bird in her arms chirps feebly. Susanna enters.

Susanna	Mother, the baby... and Margaret, too.
Anne	
Susanna	A month. This happens just a month after Judith's wedding.[7] Why? I cannot believe it. Thomas must know it all. Did Judith know?

For nine months she kept her silence.
Oh, Margaret...
Did Thomas make her a promise to marry?
Or give her money for her secrecy?
How she must have suffered as she saw her belly swelling up!

| Anne | Margaret, Judith and the baby... I pity them all. |
| Susanna | We now see why the wedding had to be performed so hurriedly. He didn't even try to get the bishop's licence, and cared not about his expulsion from the church! He was so urgent to marry Judith just to avoid the match with Margaret. And Father's money? – Was he greedy for Judith's inheritance? Love? Where did love hide away? |

---

7) Judith's wedding was February 10th, 1616; Margaret's death was March 15th.

Anne   We killed Margaret. All of us.

⟨Scene 5⟩

Will's Room

A month before Will's Death

25 March, 1616

Will is correcting his will, word by word. It is hard for him to write. A bottle of wine and a glass sit on his desk.

Will   Death is standing on the threshold. I'll willingly follow the road unknown, the road no one may refuse and from which no one returns. I will go with solemnity, like one entering a deep sleep, or as a swan elegantly on the water. I will accept my ending with full spirit.

He drinks. He frowns as if drinking poison. He sighs and goes on writing.

VO   *(Voice of Will, but clear and healthy, in contrast with* *his present voice)* I expunge Thomas Quiney from my will. I deny him all chance of inheritance. Nobody will inherit who is not my direct blood. My estate will go to Susanna and her son, and the grandson...

Will   *(old and sick voice)* I amend this because of my great disappointment in Judith. This is the only way. She will feel her father's broken heart when this will is opened.

VO   The £300, I change it to £150. She can have £50 more when the house on Chapel Lane is handed over to Susanna. If Judith's son reaches three years and is still alive, he may receive £150.

While Will is working on this, Anne enters. There is a certain distance between them and they speak individually, but their words seem to approximate a dialogue.

Anne   The Thomas Quiney scandal has left a terrible scar on us. Will is hurt most of all; he ages quickly. We have no time. I have something to say before he departs.

Will　　This house and all of my estate, I bequeath to
　　　　　Susanna. Anne? She will have one third. As a wife,
　　　　　she has a right to it, so it need not be stated in writing.
　　　　　But I wish to specify *(writes)* the second best bed.

On the screen rear wall, this part of the authentic will appears.

Anne　　What? The second best bed? He bequeaths it to
　　　　　me? What does he mean? We each have our own
　　　　　bed now, obviously. Does he mean the first bed we
　　　　　shared in the early days, in Henry Street? Surely not.
　　　　　What is it? Is he losing his mind? No, we cannot
　　　　　part this way.

Will　　The second best bed...

Anne　　Something is understood now. Your mind is as
　　　　　distant as London. Why didn't I follow you to
　　　　　London? I could have walked there even if my feet
　　　　　wore off, though you never sent for me. Our love
　　　　　was as short as a midsummer night.

Will　　My head is stopped. My memory is failing. This
　　　　　damned pain in my eyes; I cannot see well. I would
　　　　　hate to think Cordelia might know of it. It's a

loathsome thought. She deserted me... She is more disloyal to her father than Desdemona.

(drinks)

O Judith, my daughter, how you suffer, how you endure the whole ordeal. Your soul must be shattered! You should tell me. Or is this your revolt against me?

(pause)

The letters of the will on the screen expand into extreme close-up, break up into pieces, and disappear.

The reversal improperly occurs at the end of Act 5, in the final moment of my life. It usually comes in Act 3, does it not? I work it into the beginning or end of Act 3.

How wonderfully plotted! It overlaps the events of Act 1.

How superb! So original! It must be His touch. He is the great creator who completes my life with an exquisite plot! Hamlet says, "There's a divinity that shapes our ends." "O, I am fortune's fool."

Anne   I think of you always.

Will	*(raise up his head)*
Anne	I think of your lovers too.
Will	Did you say lovers? You are the first and best lover, Anne, I should say. Of course I had others after you.
Anne	
Will	Emilia Lanier was one of them. How surprised I was when Judith mentioned her name. And the Earl of Southampton was one of them too. Yes, a man, Anne. The man who occupied an exalted place in my mind. I dedicated my first poem to him. He was much younger, an innocent and graceful young man who had not experienced the rough waves of the world. Southampton was beautiful. The day we performed *Richard II*, we were unintentionally involved in Lord Essex's rebellion. Essex thought of himself as Bullingbrook... He was executed by his beloved Queen; the Queen soon died too. Henry himself was barely saved from execution. God helped him! I was deeply anxious, and urgently prayed for his life. So urgently...

(thinking)

Why is this memory so clear? Do I have time?

He stops his hands reaching for the bottle and covers his eyes with both hands.

Anne What are you talking about? You loved a man? Listen, there is no time to talk such rubbish. The end is approaching. Will, arouse your mind before we meet it.

Will My eyes... I cannot see.

The pain is getting stronger. His face falls down on the desk. He struggles. The conversation becomes more entangled. Now only Will and Anne are lit.

Will I knew... Anne, you were waiting for me here, but I had to be in London. So I gave you money instead.

Anne You gave me money for a comfortable life here. But money doesn't solve everything. You cannot be forgiven. The solitude, the loneliness was a high price for me to pay. Why didn't you bring us with you, wherever it was? Why did you leave us in such an isolated countryside? Tell me now! There is no time.

Will The word "loneliness" sounds so alien to me. I have

forgotten the feeling. I was so occupied with stages, actors, my writing, and the like. I am sorry, Anne. Solitude is necessary for a writer, of course. Do you understand when I say I could not have invented those words and worlds if I had not lived alone there?

Will is attacked again by the pain in his eyes. Anne looks at him calmly.

Anne   What a shame! You disregard me as if I don't know what writing is! Do you boast of being a successful writer, in front of me? I do not admit that it is a consequence of your own effort and ability. If I had not let you go? If I had not accepted your leaving, would it have been possible? You had a duty to live here as a husband and a father of three children.
(breathes)
What do you think filled the vacant place you left? What is theatre? The theatre you loved. It is merely a lie. The love and friendship are all counterfeit. The kings and nobles are all aped by actors. They are not real. All is untrue. Does the world become less

absurd and less miserable without your plays? No! The world is so created, in its origins. What was I in that counterfeit world of yours? What were our children in it? People say you had genius. While you found your genius, I struggled with my loneliness. I saw helplessly as my son was dying. The children have grown up under ridicule without a father. That is how we lived. Without you.

Will   Anne, you are an incorrigible, solemn Puritan.

Anne   And you are a rotten Catholic pretending to be a Protestant.

Will   A chasm between us that cannot be bridged.

Anne   It has formed an uncrossable river.

Will   Anne, recall our love when we first met. The love only we two shared.

Anne   It was a counterfeit, too, so you left.

Will   No, no, Anne. It was a gift from God. I believe I could write because I experienced that love. The love we shared, the memory engraved in our minds, gave us energy to live forward. It is precious, although it cooled. I have realized this lately.

Anne

Will   It was this love that enabled you to wait for me,

wasn't it?

Anne   Don't think that your words comfort me. To me, you are still an immature boy who never grew up.

Will   *(bitter smile)* But see? I am dying now.

Anne   Who is not? We all die.

Will   *(can't open his eyes and suffers)*

Anne   I want to ask you what you would say, if we could exchange our lives. Would you believe mine was worth living?

Light slowly fades out on Anne; it is only on Will. Will is left alone as if he is the only creature in the world. We can hear the silence. Will speaks now and then in spite of his painful eyes.

Will   Why I... left you — no, why I couldn't come back to you earlier — or rather, why I had to stay in London... Anne, you will hate me more if I say the reason. It was the beautiful young man. I was just an ordinary actor and a writer in his eyes. But he was special in mine. A great distance between us... I knew. I adored him. I wrote sonnets thinking of him. *(silence)*

When he came to see my plays, I could die for him

in delight. It was a pure happiness.

Laughs self-mockingly. Laughter and coughing are mixed.

I should have died in the fire… in the burning Globe.

Will falls down helplessly on the desk like an old scarecrow.

Henry Wriothesley, 3rd Earl of Southampton, appears upstage. With blue eyes, long auburn hair, he is a fair youth. He is in his early twenties. In his hand is a scroll, on which Will's sonnet is dedicated to him. He elegantly walks towards Will. He is looking at Will slouched on the ground. Will feels somebody is there, raises up his face, and sees the young man. He can't believe his eyes. The young man smiles. Will struggles to his feet. The young man shows the scroll and unfolds it.

The last part of Sonnet 29 appears on the screen.

VO   "and then my state
                          Like to the lark at break of day arising
                          From sullen earth sings hymns at heaven's gate;
                          For thy sweet love remember'd such wealth brings,

That then I scorn to change my state with kings."

Will hugs him for a short moment. The young man exits following the exact path from which he entered. Anne reappears wearing the black costume from Act 1. Anne and the young man cross paths and note one another at the last moment. Anne's eyes gazing at Southampton now turn to Will. She walks to Will. These movements are seen on the screen at the proper moment.

Will tries hard to walk but stumbles. He falls down again and tries to stand up. He walks unstably and the direction is unclear. Is he trying to reach Anne, or the young man? He seems to have almost lost his eyesight. The couple's movements convey the conflict and struggle between them. The feelings intensify.

Will   "Here is the journey's end."
            A blind actor stands alone.
            The exit cue is given to him, but he is lost.
            "All the world's a stage,
            And all the men and women merely players;
            They have their exits and their entrances."

Susanna and Judith enter holding wild flowers and weeds. They are dressed as in Act 1. The three women look like Lear's three daughters, and become the three weird sisters of Macbeth as time passes. They move or dance and talk as in Act 1. Will and the three women move around as though they are playing a blind game of hide-and-seek. The blind Will stumbles and tries to catch one of them. Susanna and Judith swiftly put flowers and weeds on Will's head and clothes and run away. He stumbles. The flowers and weeds fall on the stage. These are seen on the screen.

Susanna   Poor actors, we are "walking shadows" on a stage.

Judith   "All the world's a stage,

And we are merely players;

We have our exits and entrances."

We are so many puppets.

Anne   Don't leave this way.

We have something to discuss.

You listen to what I have in mind to say to you.

My words --

Susanna   … Words.

Judith   Words. Words in her deeper mind.

Will   Alack!… A… A… nne…

Will's spirit is very confused and his life is burned out like a candle.

He stumbles and stumbles, looking like Lear on the heath. He murmurs and shouts, and tears his clothes. He is a blind old man. Flowers and weeds are falling down.

Will   "You see me here, you gods, a poor old man,

As full of grief as age, wretched in both.

You think I'll weep,

No I'll not weep."

Judith   I didn't want to live like mother...

(cynical and vain laughter)

But I realize I have merely followed the road she walked.

Did Margaret die on my behalf?

She was buried with the dreams she took away from me.

I lament that I did not go to London alone.

Alone, alone, alone.

The world prohibits women from doing anything "alone."

The world makes women fear being alone.

You should have let me go, although the world forbids it.

For me to try my fortune in the world.

Susanna	A ship is coming.
	We have to cross the river.
	"The undiscovered country, from whose bourn
	No traveller returns."
Judith	"When we are born, we cry that we are come to this
	great stage of fools" – do we not?
Susanna	A drum, a drum, it doth come,
	River fog gets thicker,
	Wind blows
Judith	Wind blows.
Will	"Blow, winds, and crack your cheeks!
	Rage, blow,"
Judith	The bubbles and fog of the river vanish into air,
	Sun appears through rain and clouds.
Susanna	"So foul and fair a day!"
Susanna/Judith	"Fair is foul, and foul is fair."
Judith	Where shall we return to,
	When our last breath shall vanish into air?
Anne	"Sleep that knits up the ravelled sleeves of care,
	The death of each day's life, sore labour's bath,
	Balm of hurt minds, great nature's second course,
	Chief nourishment in life's feast."
Will	The end...

Judith	Sleep…
Susanna	"To die, to sleep…"

Will falls down. The women move towards him; they are aware of his death. Anne steps back, standing apart from the rest of them.

Judith	Father, Father, You left for the world, but I never found a way…
Susanna	Farewell…
	The ship must leave
	Out the light,
	Down the curtain

Music fades in and out. Susanna comes forward. Anne stands up straight alone. Her hand is shaking.
Judith mourns, holding Will's hands.

Susanna The breath stops. The end arrives finally like this. The twenty-third of April. Poetry, plays, and a will are all he left behind. He obsessively left nothing else, as though hiding himself from this world. Even his manuscripts do not exist. Why? What was he afraid of?

Did he wish to protect himself from this world of the Protestants, because he was a recusant? His descendants someday in the future might be irresistibly seized by a strong doubt as to whether he was a real author at all. This doubt will rather enlarge his existence and attract the world to him even more. Did he also imagine and contrive this consequence beforehand? I am suspicious.

Judith   Was he a husband? The man named Thomas Quiney one day disappeared leaving three sons to me. Nobody knows where, when and how he lived and died. I heard once that someone saw him in London. How is it that he could go, by himself, where he wanted to go, whereas I could never go, let alone by myself. I was deserted.

Susanna   Mother passed away several years after Father's death, the very year Father's first folio was published. She never saw it, unfortunately or fortunately. I, Susanna Hall, died at age sixty-six. Judith Quiney died at seventy-seven. She lived longer than I but spent her life in extreme loneliness. Father is buried inside Holy Trinity Church; so is Mother. Not together, but beside him. John and I are also buried

inside the church, beside Father. Judith was buried in the graveyard outside, though no evidence remains. Hamnet's grave has also disappeared; his death was so long ago. Everything departs...
"Golden lads and girls all must,
As chimney-sweepers, come to dust."

Anne All we foolish humans want

is

a sleep that is balm to hurt minds,

that nourishes life's feast, and that

is

the journey's end.

End of Play

이지훈 한영판 희곡집

여로의 끝 (*The Promised End*)

초판 1쇄 인쇄일   2023년 9월 7일
초판 1쇄 발행일   2023년 9월 16일

지 은 이   이지훈
영어번역   이지훈
만 든 이   이정옥
만 든 곳   평민사
　　　　　서울시 은평구 수색로 340 〈202호〉
　　　　　전화 : 02) 375-8571   팩스 : 02) 375-8573
　　　　　http://blog.naver.com/pyung1976
이 메 일   pyung1976@naver.com
등록번호   25100-2015-000102호
　ISBN   978-89-7115-092-4   03800
정 　 가   12,000원

2020 아르코 창작산실 연극 대본 공모 선정작